SUMMER BREAK FAE

Uncle Chip Saves the Fae

Book 4

JAMIE DAVIS

Summer Break Fae

By Jamie Davis

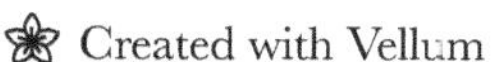 Created with Vellum

Acknowledgments

This book made possible with the generous assistance of these Kickstarter Backers:

Samantha Ghormley, Melissa Showers, maileguy, Eva Holmquist, Samantha Newberry, John Idlor, Joe Gillis, Juanita J Nesbitt, E.M. Middel, Stephen Ballentine, RJ Hopkinson, Philip T Davis, Gerald P. McDaniel, Nicole Anderson, Michael Jenck, Sheryl R. Hayes, Russell Ventimeglia, Mary Barzee, Trudie Nesbitt, Dominick Graham, Sven Lugar, Janis Ossmann, Joyce Casement, Dead Fish Books, Tina, Ronald L Weston, Kristi Preston-Barnes, Palle Rosendahl Rømer, Rebecca Hodgkins, Rabbi Fred Natkin, Vicki Sinnett, Cindy Fortenberry, Penny Noble, Jim Gotaas, Cheryl Miller, Laura Ware, Karina Krogh, Katy Board, Troy Hill, Christian "Mecki" Hejl, Pam Ripperda, Will It Work, Ariane Beauparlant

Rose

Cold spray blew across the shingled beach stones, dampening my hair and plastering stray strands to my cheek where they escaped the hood of my raincoat. I suppressed a shiver and used a little of my precious magical mana to cast a charm against the chill coming off the North Sea.

As my eyes pierced the foggy night's gloom, my Fae sight cut through the darkness. I stared at the stone seawall and the path behind it, tracking the shadowed figure coming toward the small patio where I crouched behind a picnic table. I pulled at the shadows around the back of the metal table. I didn't want to be seen.

The approaching person was taller than I'd expected. My sources said they were a fairy or low Fae. Unlike the high Fae, who were sometimes named elves in the misguided lore of humans, the simpler fairy folk tended to be smaller and slight of build. If the information I had was correct, this particular fairy was a giant among their kind.

I shifted my crouched position to the side and caught the corner of the metal bench with my kneecap. Pain shot through my left knee and down my leg. Before I could stop myself, I drew in a hissing breath.

The figure paused only a dozen yards away, and the darkened shadows of their hood turned in my direction. A man's voice, thick with a highland Scottish brogue, said, "Who's there? Come out and show yourself."

I held still, hoping my hold on the surrounding shadows was enough to keep me hidden. I wanted to follow this person, not challenge them on the beach of this coastal Scottish town.

The man pulled his right hand from his pocket and raised it up, palm outward in my direction. He snapped his fingers, and a glowing globe of white light about the size of a softball floated toward me. The magical energy of his casting pressed hard against my cloak of shadows, giving me a taste of his dark power. His mystical strength might have outmatched my own. On the plus side, at least it illuminated him so I could see better. The trimmed salt-and-pepper beard and mustache framed an older man's face creased with age and concern.

The shadows around me melted back as the globe drifted closer and closer. Beads of sweat popped up on my forehead despite the cold sea winds blowing on my face. I was losing my hold on the magical shadows. Light magic almost always overpowered shadow magic, and his strength with the dark forces made it even easier for him.

I released the spell and stood, my hand gripping the hilt of my sword beneath my long, gray raincoat.

"Who are you?" the man asked. His floating light stopped six feet away from me, lighting up my face in the gloom. "What are you doing lurking out here in the night?"

"I'm waiting for you, actually." Sometimes, simple honesty could disarm an opponent.

"You're an American? I don't know anyone from your country." He paused and tilted his head back while he sniffed at the air. A wry grin twisted the corners of his mouth upward. "You're Fae, not a human witch. What do you want with me?"

"I traced you from your posts on a dark web chatroom. You talked about having a vision that revealed the new Fae Queen to you."

"Bah, that? I was just messing with the conspiracy types who hang out there. It wasn't real."

He was lying. Warren, my investigator, had a series of search queries scraping the web for keywords. This guy's posts had come too close to be accidental. He'd either actually had a vision of my niece,

Sadie, or knew someone who had. I didn't fail to notice his left hand dipping into the cloak's folds. What was he hiding?

"You said the new queen would be found in the minster of the west in the New World. That she'd appear ordinary and live amongst the mundanes. Where did you see or hear that description?"

The man barked a laugh. "I knew it." He crowed at the moon before returning his gaze to me. "She's real and in America, like I said." His right hand pointed at me. "And you know who she is."

I readied myself for the inevitable confrontation. There was just one piece of important information I needed before I dealt with him.

"So, it was you who had the vision? You saw the future queen?"

His mouth twitched in a frown. "I might have seen it, or I might have heard it from someone. That you're here now tells me all I need to know. Her growing power is breaking through the veil that has hidden her from those who seek her. It's only a matter of time before we narrow our search enough to identify her."

I had worried this would come someday, though I'd wished for a few more years before Sadie was discovered. Her increased command of the powerful forces at her beck and call must have breached our family's long-standing wards, put in place to hide her and our entire line.

The shadow man brought out his left hand from the cloak, gripping something in his fist. He held out his hands and cupped them together. A soft, deep-red glow leaked from between his fingers. "I sent a team to the States over ten years ago. They followed the clues in an obscure line I found in a forgotten prophecy. I put little faith in them discovering anything until they disappeared without a trace after reporting a successful hit on a minor noble family. I never followed up on it, assuming the Unusual community in America had snapped them up. I see now that was a mistake."

I froze, quivering with anger. Had this man been the one who'd ordered Lili and Bobby's deaths all those years ago? My teeth ground together. He had to be stopped.

No. He had to die!

I snarled my battle cry and charged at him. My sword swung from its scabbard at my side. I lunged up and over the table, using my magic to propel my leap forward.

My blade clove through the space where he'd stood only a second before. I landed in a half crouch. He wasn't there.

A booming laugh from the darkness to my left warned me he'd projected his image forward on the sea path. I had been a fool to fall for his illusion. Now I was going to pay.

With my free hand, I swept up the edge of the long raincoat. I'd imbued it with a charm of protection earlier. I hoped it would be enough.

The glowing ember of magical energy the man held in his cupped hands erupted outward in my direction. At this range, he couldn't miss. It grew in size until it was as big as a grapefruit and impacted on my raised coat.

My impromptu shield crumbled into burning ash around me. The spell's explosion blasted me off my feet, and I landed nearly ten feet away. Gravel beside the concrete path dug into my exposed and now-burned skin. Pain seared through me as I struggled to regain control. He'd easily pierced my protections.

I pushed past the pain and bounded to my feet, lucky to have kept a grip on my blade. I adjusted my path to his true location and charged back.

He laughed and sent another energy ball at me.

This time, I was ready. I swept my magical blade in an arc, intercepting the captured globe of heated plasma. My natural magic drew in power from the chill air and misting rain around me. I vented it out through the sword to dissipate the energy inside the spell.

It was my turn to laugh. "You won't catch me unawares again. I've searched for you at least as long as you've searched for us."

"Let me guess, my team killed someone you loved. A friend, a lover, perhaps?"

I growled. "She was my sister, my best friend. She didn't deserve the end you sent after her. Know this. I'm the reason your acolyte never returned to you."

He walked in an arc away from the seawall, keeping the distance between us constant. "You have genuine power, then. My resources in the States were formidable."

I shifted to follow his movements. "A witch and a few weretigers weren't much of a challenge. Though they took the secret of who paid them to the grave."

"Well, now you know who to thank. If your sister was the one who died, then you should have risen to her place. That makes you the one I've been searching for."

I almost missed a step. He thought I was the heir to the Fae Queen's throne. That meant he didn't know about Sadie. She was still hidden, at least for now. I needed to end him and the threat he posed before he discovered anything else. As she got older and more power-ful, Sadie would eventually reveal herself to all, no matter what we did to hide her away.

"Yes," I said, standing tall. "You've found me at last. Come and finish the job, if you dare."

The man clapped his hands together. A thunderous blast lanced down from the sky.

I dove to the side, narrowly avoiding the called lightning and the crater it blasted in the gravel. My hand pushed down, and I completed my roll and regained my feet in time to counter the incoming blow from the ironshod club he produced from behind him.

My blade drew a shower of sparks from his magically charged weapon. I didn't fear him. My sword had power, too.

I pushed aside the club, causing it to thump into the ground beside me. Then I recovered with a riposte and lunge at his midsection.

Somehow, he twisted to the side, and my sword met thin air, though I ripped through his black leather cloak as he whirled away from my attack.

"You are a challenge." His tongue flicked out as if he were a snake tasting the air. He cocked his head to the side and chuckled. "No, you're not the one I seek. Your magic doesn't have the taste, the wild energy of the one I have sensed in the distance. Your ruse did not work." He raised his hand in a gesture of runic traveling. "I will not be sidetracked."

Realizing he'd discovered my lie, I drew in all my power and funneled it into a single thrust at his back. I was already overextended, but I didn't have a choice. I couldn't let him get away.

My sword glowed, incandescent in the deep, rainy gloom by the seawall. The magic exploded out in a wave of crackling heat that should have seared through his protections. The sword's tip passed by, striking nothing. There was no one there. I swung around searching for him, but he was gone, his runic spell taking him somewhere else.

I collapsed onto the sidewalk, gasping for breath. I'd spent physical power as well as my remaining mana stores in that attack. And it was all for nothing. The rain pelted down harder as I rolled onto my back. It didn't matter. My raincoat was a tattered wreck of ash and singed fabric across my shoulders. Not enough remained of it to shield me from even a thin drizzle, let alone the North Sea's storm-driven rain, now pressing in on the seaside town of Stonehaven.

I didn't know how long I lay there on the concrete, soaking up the water through every inch of my clothing all the way to my skin. A shiver passed through me. *That's enough, Rose. Get ahold of yourself.*

A dog barked in the distance, near the buildings along the strand of beach skirting the town's old harbor. I had to get moving. Unlike my adversary, I couldn't snap up a rune of traveling and disappear. If I wanted to get back to protect those I loved, I had to catch an early flight out of Aberdeen, get to London, and fly back to the United States.

I didn't think the warlock—or whatever he was—could make the trip all the way across the Atlantic with a simple rune spell. There was still a chance I could catch up with him and make it home before he arrived to track down Sadie. I had to get her away from home for a little while until her magic dissipated some.

Puberty was hard enough without having to wrestle with wild Fae magic and everything that came with it at the same time. Thirteen-year-old Sadie had a lot to learn about controlling her burgeoning powers as well as reining in her headstrong pre-teen emotions. It would be best to deal with that away from home.

I sat up, ignoring the growing force of the wind and rain on my face. I leaned to the side, and my hand passed across something thin and round on the concrete beneath me. Holding the disc up, I peered at it in the deepening gloom. The wooden talisman coin was ringed in black iron, a black and red runic design carved on either side. I didn't recognize the runes or the intricate way they interlocked inside the pattern. My adversary had dropped it when he escaped.

I slipped it into my pocket for later investigation and pulled out my phone. I looked up the contact I needed and tapped the icon to place the call.

The phone rang twice before they picked up on the other end.

"Mistress Rose," Taren said. "I didn't expect to hear from you so soon after your arrival in Scotland. Is there a problem with the accommodations I arranged for you?"

"No, Taren, the suite at the hotel is fine." My dig-master had traveled the world with me on my many archeological adventures over the years. I often used him to make travel arrangements for me. "I've completed my business here earlier than expected and need to push up my flight arrangements to go home."

"Oh, my. It's late in the evening, but let me pull up the British Airways site and see what I can do."

"Thank you. I'm headed back to the hotel to pack up now. Get me something leaving first thing in the morning if you can. I don't care if I have to sit in the center seat. Speed is of the essence, not comfort."

"Is everything all right, Mistress? If there's something I can help with, you only have to ask."

"No, I just need to get home. Text me the flight details once you've arranged everything." I hung up and suppressed a shiver as a gust of icy wind off the North Sea whipped past me. I was a wet mess and had to get back to my rental car to get warm again. I used up the bit of reserves I had left to keep the dangerous chill at bay. A long shower and some food would go a long way to help me recover. I also needed to inspect the burns on my arm, though my Fae charm necklace's fire protections had staved off the worst of that initial attack when the raincoat had failed.

There wasn't much open all night in this part of the country, but I was sure I could find something on my way back to Aberdeen. If not, I had some energy bars back in my suite. They would do well enough in a pinch. I could always grab something at the airport in the morning.

2

Chip

The line of cars moved through the parking lot at a snail's pace as students emerged from Westside Middle School. I resisted the urge to give in to my old New York sensibilities and blow the horn. Suburban parents frowned on such crass behavior. Besides, Sadie would be out of school soon enough.

My attention was so focused ahead in the line that I missed Sadie coming around behind the SUV. She popped open the door and climbed into the passenger side.

"Hey, kiddo. Ready for some sparring?"

Sadie crossed her arms and slumped down in her seat. "Do we have to go to the dojo? I don't feel like sparring today."

"You know your Aunt Rose made us both promise to keep up with our practice sessions while she was gone. I'm not getting on her bad side because we didn't put in the time in the dojo together. Come on, it'll be fun."

Sadie ducked down farther when Astrid Heraty and another girl walked past toward a car farther back in the line. I caught myself before I waved hello. I prided myself on reading Sadie's moodiness of late. There was no telling what was going on between her and Astrid, another of the hidden Fae Unusuals attending this mundane school. I had to let her work things out on her own. My middle school memories were muddled, but I distinctly remembered experiencing personal doubts on the inside even though I was pretty popular. I'd keep an eye on her, but whatever was going on, Sadie would figure it out.

The line ahead moved forward, and I followed the other cars out through the parking lot and headed toward Main Street. The dojo had a private sparring area in addition to its lucrative after-school care and training program. Rose had it booked three days a week right after school.

"Perk up. We can hit the cafe on the way home for an iced latte if you want." Sadie liked it when I let her get what Rose and I referred to as big girl drinks. We didn't want her getting hooked on coffee quite this early, but the occasional order as a reward wasn't out of bounds.

"Yeah, I guess that's okay." Sadie stared out the passenger window without glancing my way.

"I'll even let you pick the weapons for sparring. You love it when I let you choose what we'll work on."

"That's only because you always choose the sword. It's soooo ordinary."

Without glancing in her direction, I could picture her eyes rolling.

"Okay, so what'll we work on today?" I pulled to a stop at an inter-section and looked over at her. "Your pick."

"Knife and buckler." She didn't even hesitate.

I suppressed a sigh. Sadie's martial skills had grown as fast as she had. Her inherited human athleticism from the Proctor side, coupled with her Fae royal ancestry, gave her unexpected speed, strength, and grace throughout her combat drills.

She was crazy quick with her feet and hands. In close combat exercises such as knife and buckler, she was unmatched, even though she was only thirteen. Even Rose was hard-pressed to beat her when it came to raw speed and quickness.

I forced a smile onto my face. "Knife and buckler it is, sweetie. We'll work out some of whatever is going on in your life."

"Whatevs." She pulled her phone out of her pocket and ignored me the rest of the drive to the training dojo.

I wasn't sure what to do with the new moody teen version of my niece. She used to be so cheerful and open with me when I picked her up at school. That had changed over the last year, as if seventh grade had infused her with angst and darkness.

The drive through town to the martial arts school took a long, silent ten minutes. At the strip mall, I pulled into a parking spot in front and got out. I opened the back of the SUV and grabbed both gym bags. I held the one I had packed for Sadie out for her.

Sadie stared at me. "I really don't feel like doing this, Uncle Chip. Do we have to?"

"It's only an hour." I tried to find a silver lining for her to focus on. "Tell you what. When Miss Ellie drops off your brother in a half hour, I'll let you stop and start on your homework while I work with him. Deal?"

"Yeah, okay." She took the bag and slipped the strap over her shoulder.

We walked inside, and I waved at the owner, a retired army type from one of the special forces groups. He was also a half-minotaur, though I'd never seen him out of his human form.

"Hey, Chip," Barry said. "The room downstairs is ready for you. Let me know if you need anything. I'll be up here with the kids here for their regular lessons."

"Thanks, dude." I hooked a thumb at my niece. "Sadie can't wait to get started."

She rolled her eyes, grunted, and made a beeline for the women's locker room. Barry and I shared a look before I went into the men's side to change into my sweats and tank top.

I waited downstairs for almost five minutes before Sadie finally came down. Rather than comment on her making me wait, I pointed over at the practice weapons on the rack by the mirrored wall.

"I already picked mine. There's another dagger and buckler combination over there for you." I'd picked the lighter of the two sets, leaving her the weighted versions. It was my hope the extra workout would dig her out of the doldrums.

I stepped into the middle of the training mat and crouched in my ready pose. Sadie picked up the wooden dagger and dinner-plate sized metal buckler. She hefted them for a second and turned her head to stare at me. She knew I'd left her the heavier ones. Her brows lowered with a determined glare that left me wondering if I'd made the right decision.

Sadie twisted her wrist, twirling the wooden dagger around in a circle as she tested its weight and balance. She stopped a few feet away from me and squared off.

I nodded a bow, which she returned. Before I could blink, she lunged in, stretching to her full extension with the dagger's tip aimed right at my midsection.

My buckler came across on instinct alone, honed from long hours practicing against Rose. I barely blocked the incoming blade.

I realized it was a feint too late to bring my dagger up to counter her buckler. She twisted her arm and punched the metal knob in the center of the shield into my shoulder.

I staggered back, grunting at the force behind the punching blow. My dagger batted away two more thrusts from her wooden dagger. Then the two bucklers smashed together. I used my greater strength and mass to stop her charge before she forced me off the edge of the practice mat.

As we came face to face, she drove her dagger in from the side. The blunted tip came in hard and slid across the ribs under my right arm.

The pain of the full-strength blow drove the air from my lung, and I oofed when the breath came out of my mouth. Rose had taught her well. Sadie fought in here like it was the real thing, and she was old enough now to leave big-girl bruises on her uncle.

I twisted around, using our locked bucklers to spin her with me until she had her back at the mat's edge. With a yank, I disengaged and backpedaled to the center of the mat. It was time to think about landing a few hits of my own. I didn't want to hurt her, but she needed to learn a lesson or two here as well.

"Nice shot." I stretched my buckler up high in the air and leaned to the side to stretch out the sore spot along my side. "You won't score another one that easily."

"We'll see." Sadie charged in at me.

This time I thrust out with my mind, creating a knee-high barrier with my invisible Guardian's shield.

The trick worked. She tripped and landed sprawled on the floor at my feet.

I leaned down to tap her back with my blade to prove I'd won the point.

Sadie rolled to the side while reaching out with her buckler hand. Two fingers extended from the shield's handle to point up at me. Her sapphire-blue eyes flared with magic.

I was already leaning forward, and the spell-charged tug pulled me completely off balance. The yelp escaped my mouth right before she punched up with her dagger and caught me in the shoulder on my way down.

The wooden dagger dug into my muscle, sending a shooting pain down my entire arm. It failed to support my weight when I landed on it, and I collapsed to the floor on my face.

Sadie rolled up and straddled my back, jabbing me twice in the right kidney hard enough to make me see stars.

I groaned and bucked upward from my prone position. The sudden move knocked Sadie to the side and allowed me to climb up to my feet. I faced her across the mat as she stood.

"I just killed you three times, Uncle Chip. That should be enough."

My bruised ribs and aching side agreed with her, but I would not give in. She still had a hint of snarky darkness in her tone. I needed to work that out of her and get her to talk to me.

"I don't know what's bugging you, Sadie Proctor, but if you think I'm going to go away just because of a few bruises, you don't know me very well."

Her eyes narrowed, and she huffed at me.

I charged in, then dodged to the left in a feint that drew her into stabbing at my exposed and injured side.

My feet twisted in place, pulling my body around so her strike slid right by me. I brought my buckler down on her extended wrist.

Sadie squawked, and her hand spasmed, sending the dagger spinning to the floor.

I used a move I had learned the hard way from Sadie's Aunt Rose and buried my left knee in Sadie's side. This time it was her turn to stagger backward. I followed with my wooden dagger. When she fell to the ground, I landed next to her on one knee with my dagger at her throat.

She hissed, breathing hard, and stared up at me. "That hurt."

"It was supposed to. Your aunt always says to practice the way we'd have to fight. Would she have held back?"

Sadie's eyes turned away for a second. "No. She'd have smacked me with the dagger, too."

"Exactly. What's the lesson here?" I stood and reached down to give her a hand up.

Instead of taking the offered help, she kicked up with her feet, rolling backward and coming up to stand well away from me.

"I wasn't going to attack again," I said. "I was helping you up."

"Never trust an opponent until the fight is over. She says that, too."

I smiled. "Fair enough. Okay, the fight is over. Now, will you please tell me what's got you all twisted in a knot today?"

A devious half-grin crossed her face. Then, just as quickly, she frowned. "It's Astrid. I asked her about this kid in our math section she's been hanging out with."

"Oh, a boy, then."

She glared at me. "Do you want to know what's bugging me or not, Uncle Chip?"

"Sorry, go ahead."

Sadie kicked her foot at the ground. "Well, Astrid lied and told him I was asking about him. Then he turned my way and pretended to stick his finger down his throat. Like I made him sick."

"Astrid's your friend. Why did she do that to you?"

"Lately, she's been acting weird and hanging out with girls we never liked before. They told her to do it. I'm so angry and… and…"

"Embarrassed? I think it's time you and I had a talk about something important. About boys."

"Ewww, no, Uncle Chip." Sadie held up her hand and turned away from me. "Aunt Rose already had the talk with me. I don't need you to do it, too."

"This is a different talk about boys. You see, boys at your age aren't as grown up as you are. They're mostly still little kids inside and don't know when they really like anyone, at least not that way. That and they're just plain stupid. Wait until they're a few years older and have some maturity. Eventually, they understand their emotions the same way you do. Does that make sense?"

"I think so. You're saying I shouldn't be interested in seventh grade boys. Don't worry, there's no danger in that, at least not now."

"Good," I said. "See, Uncle Chip has some useful advice after all."

Sadie turned back to me and smiled. "So, I should aim higher and start looking for someone among the ninth graders who wait at the bus stop with us." She nodded. "That makes so much more sense. Plus, it'll avoid someone Astrid will know, so she can't mess it up for me again." Sadie skipped over, picked up her wooden dagger, and stretched up to give me a peck on the cheek. "Thanks, Uncle Chip, that was really helpful."

She crossed the training room to replace the dagger and buckler. Then she picked up her gym bag and bounced up the steps to the locker rooms.

I realized my mouth was open, and I closed it before I said something that would make the situation any worse. How had she taken what I'd said and turned it into focusing on high school boys? Rose was going to have a fit when she heard about this. Sadie talked to her about everything, and I was sure she'd tell Aunt Rose all about Uncle Chip's brilliant advice.

My phone alarm went off on the table by the door. It was time to go up and meet Ellie when she dropped off Addy from the elementary school. I returned my weapons to the rack and started up the stairs. I had to walk back what I'd said to Sadie, but I honestly did not know how.

3

Rose

Reston, my Aunt Allura's butler, pulled open the door of the family mansion and stepped back to let me in. "Good day, Mistress Rose. I passed along the message you sent to your aunt from the airport. She's waiting upstairs in her drawing room."

"Thanks, Reston. I know it's close to dinner. Tell Mrs. McGarry this might take a while and interfere with Aunt Allura's dinner."

"I'll let the cook know. Thank you for the warning. Of course, you could stay for dinner and discuss what you need over the evening meal."

I laughed and gestured to my denim jacket, T-shirt, and blue jeans. "I'm not dressed for dinner with my aunt. I'd never get a word in edge-wise around her comments about my attire for the meal."

Reston hid the barest hint of a grin behind a small cough. "Very well. I'll tell the cook to keep things warm until you come down."

"Thank you." There was also the way dinner conversation always turned to many other family matters. If I went up to the drawing room, I could keep the discussion targeted on my original topic and use the impending dinner hour to keep it from devolving into other items.

I headed up the broad main stairs off the entry hall to the second floor. Aunt Allura's drawing room was to the right at the top of the stairs. I had barely stepped off the staircase when my aunt's voice echoed down the hallway.

"Do hurry up, Rose. It's almost dinnertime."

My shoulders drooped. I had to stop for a beat and compose myself. Whenever I faced my aunt, I felt like I was a little girl who had gotten caught with her hand in the cookie jar again. It didn't matter that I was well over thirty years old and was the family's battle mistress.

Resetting my shoulders, I raised my head and strode down the hallway to the drawing room entrance.

Allura lounged on a long velvet divan. She held a hardcover, leather-bound book, though I couldn't make out the title before she closed it and set it on the seat beside her.

"Hello, Rose. How did your jaunt to Scotland work out? I recall you were most anxious about what you hoped to discover there."

"Hello, Aunt Allura. That is the reason I'm here. I came straight from the airport."

The elder Fae matriarch pursed her lips. "Am I to assume you discovered that which you sought when you left us so suddenly last week?"

"I did." I left out the part about how I wasn't exactly sure what or who it was I'd found.

Allura leaned forward and lifted her china teacup. "Do start at the beginning, my dear. You left so suddenly, none of us knew what it was you were after exactly."

"Right," I replied, feeling just like the little schoolgirl again. "Okay, ever since Lili and Bobby died, I've had some routine searches out there with a few trusted investigators. Warren has handled coordinating their regular reports, though most have turned up very little that is helpful. It's been almost ten years. I was sure we'd have someone make an attempt on Sadie again after we defeated the witch and the weretigers."

"It has been strangely quiet since that incident. Perhaps you really didn't nip out the entire plot in one swoop?"

I shook my head. "I never thought that. That's why I kept the investigations open. Last week, Warren got a report from a source in the U.K. about a release of great magical power up along the north-eastern coast of Scotland."

Allura leaned forward. "Where exactly was this?"

"Stonehaven."

My aunt frowned. "I see. The whole Dunnottar debacle has come back to haunt us, I see."

"That's what I thought, too. The only way to be sure was to go there and put eyes on the person behind all the power and find out why it was focused there. It could have been a coincidence. After all, it's been five centuries since the family went into hiding and left that castle for the New World."

Aunt Allura sipped from her cup. "Since you're here, it obviously wasn't a coincidence at all, was it?"

"No, though I wasn't able to pin down exactly who was behind the source of power. I encountered… someone. But I'm not sure who, or what, they were. Only that they were searching for the lost Fae royal line that disappeared from that area years before."

"And you think this person figured it out?"

I nodded. "I exchanged—well, let's call it—words with them, and they have sensed a corresponding surge of power here on the east coast of the United States."

Allura shook her head and gave a little smile. "But they haven't pinpointed it yet."

"No, but it will only be a matter of time. Sadie has reached that age where the wild magic within her has started bubbling to the surface at awkward times. I've tried to instill the necessary will to impose some control over her feelings, but…"

Allura sighed and set the teacup down. "But her emotional human half is not as easy to get a handle on."

"Exactly." I searched for an excuse that would explain how I'd let this get out of hand. "I remember when I was that age, and Lili, too. You weren't exactly great at keeping us in check when it came to our stronger emotions and magical energy."

"It's not the same, Rose, and you know it. Sadie has much more raw energy available to her as she comes into the full power of the Fae throne. Her abilities will soon eclipse yours, and she must be ready to exert complete control over them."

"I know. The problem is she's not ready to face anyone who challenges her claim to the throne. Especially not a sorcerer of this kind of power. He easily countered me when I tried to stop him."

Allura stood beside the divan. "Get ahold of yourself, Rose. We always knew there would be powerful forces who'd come after our girl. We can't afford to let a random escape of her wild magic expose her this soon. This place must remain a haven for a little bit longer."

"I agree. But what do we do to keep her hidden?"

Allura's grin chilled me to the bone. "We don't. In fact, we let it out for the world to see. Just not here."

"But anywhere she goes, they'll track her signature. Nowhere is as safe as it is here. We've taken too much time to set up the wards to protect the family."

"There are other things afoot that may help us kill two birds with one spell." Allura crossed to a rolltop desk against the far wall. She lifted the top and pulled out an ornate golden envelope with deep blue ribbon impressed under an azure wax seal. "This came for us the other day. I had thought to put it off to another time, but perhaps now is the time, after all."

"Time for what?" I asked. "Who is that from?"

"The Atlantic Shelf Mer King reached out and wishes to host a coming out party. It seems his granddaughter has just reached her thirteenth year, same as our Sadie. We could accept his invitation for Sadie to attend and present her to him at that time."

My eyes widened. "The Mer King knows about Sadie?"

"Our family would never have made the crossing to this new world safely without the help of the Sea Fae and their royal line. They have kept our secret all these years on the promise of a pact of cooperation once the new queen ascended to the throne."

The long game played by the Mer royal line in keeping that secret amazed me. "And we're sure they've been loyal to us the whole time? Maybe they're part of the problem we face."

Allura shook her head. "Think, Rose. They know exactly who we are and where we live. If they'd turned on us, we'd have been fending off attacks continuously since Sadie's birth. That is exactly why we must honor the King's request to meet her in person. We cannot afford to give him an excuse to change allegiances."

"We can't just take her to him and announce her at this party. It will expose her identity to all who reside in his court. It would reveal her to too many who don't know who we are. We cannot allow that."

"No, I suppose that would be precipitous." Allura paused and stared off into the distance. A smile lifted the corners of her mouth. "However, if the event were open to all young Unusual girls of that age, then we could attend in a group with others and arrange for a quick and private audience with His Majesty without letting anyone know who Sadie really is."

"I don't know," I replied. "That's taking a big chance on exposing her at a time when we know at least one enemy is tracking her."

"That's what makes this the perfect solution, my dear." Aunt Allura fanned herself with the envelope. "All the powerful beings assembled for a big gathering event would mask our girl, and anyone lurking in the shadows won't be able to pinpoint which of the many people present are the source of any potential wild magic released while she's in attendance."

I saw the possibilities in what my aunt proposed, if we could make such an important meeting happen. "What kind of pull do you have with the Mer King? We'd have to expand the initiation to include enough people of power to mask our girl's nascent abilities rising to the surface."

Allura tapped her chin with the edge of the gilded envelope. "The Mer King draws most of his power from the wild magic of the Gulf Stream, where it passes near the coast along the Carolinas. The power surging there should help to cover up any eruptions that get out of hand."

I said, "That would work. Will he be amenable to expanding the invitation to so many others?"

Allura let out a laugh with a joyful tone I'd never heard before. "The Mer King and I go way back. I think he would be happy to offer me a favor if I were to ask, especially to show off his granddaughter."

"Way back, huh?" I smiled, seeing a softer side of the stern elder aunt I'd always known.

"Leave it alone, Rose. Suffice it to say, I wasn't always the grand family matriarch I am today. I was quite the catch in my day, often more in demand than my older sister was. I turned the eye of many a young prince."

"What should I do?" I asked. "I'll need to tell Chip about this eventually. He needs to know about the risk to Sadie and what we're planning."

"Hold off while I reach out to my old friend. The school year is only a week away from being over. Nudge the Guardian to take an extended summer vacation at the seashore."

"I can do that. Any particular location? We'll want to be close to wherever the Mer King is holding court."

"I believe he summers off the region around Myrtle Beach. It was always among his favorites of the coastal settlements there, and the passage of the Gulf Stream nearby offers many opportunities for sport and adventure."

I had my phone out and searched for places to stay in that city. There were many options available. "Okay, I'll figure this out and work on getting Chip to go along with all of it. He doesn't need to know all the reasons why for now."

"Good girl." Allura reached out and pulled a long satin bell cord hanging from the ceiling. A distant chime sounded elsewhere in the grand home. "Will you be staying for dinner? I'm sure Mrs. McGarry has enough to offer you a seat at the table."

"No, I just got back into town. I need to unpack and check in with Warren and then Chip." I followed Allura out and down the stairs to the front entry hall.

"Good evening to you, then, my dear. I'll be in touch once I work out the details with my old friend on the coast."

She left me there by the door with Reston standing beside me.

He watched her leave, then said, "Am I mistaken, or was there a slight twinkle in the Mistress's eye?"

I kept my aunt's confidence. "You'll have to ask her. I've given up on trying to read her moods. Take it easy, Reston. I'll see you again soon, I'm sure."

"Good day, Mistress Rose."

I left and climbed into my Firebird. I needed to get to my apartment and unpack. Then I needed a long, hot shower and some rest. I'd call Warren first in the morning and then Chip.

4

Chip

The last day of the school year arrived. Sadie had several art projects to bring home, so I parked the SUV in the middle school lot rather than getting in the usual pickup line. A deep blue sedan backed in right next to my driver's door. I waited to let the other person get out first since I wasn't in a huge hurry. School hadn't been dismissed yet.

I jumped when someone tapped on my window. I turned and pressed the button to lower it.

"Hey, Chip," Patty Peyton said. "I feel like you've been avoiding me."

I forced my eyes to remain up away from the low-cut blouse as she leaned in. "I'm giving you your space. You asked for that after we agreed to take a break the last time we were together."

"That was over a year ago," she said. "I hoped we would still stay friends."

I thought about Sadie and her recent troubles with Patty's daughter, Astrid. It wouldn't do for her to see me out here talking to Astrid's mom.

"Patty, you're aware our girls aren't getting along right now, right?"

"Astrid mentioned something about hanging with another group of girls. Maybe your Sadie should try harder to fit in with a more popular crowd."

Her matter-of-fact tone annoyed the hell out of me. I reached for the door latch to get out and go inside the school.

Patty stepped back to make room for me. "Why, Chip, have you been working out?" She reached up and brushed her fingers across my shoulder and down my arm.

Her touch revived some pleasant memories of past trysts and a few goosebumps along my forearm. The part of my mind that always geolocated Sadie bounced back to the front, though. I remembered where my true priority lay.

"I think we should stay where we are now, Patty. Things are difficult for Sadie, and I don't want to confuse her even more with a relationship between us. You understand."

"Oh, I suppose so." Patty pushed out her lower lip in a pout. "If you change your mind, you know how to reach me." Her phone chirped and interrupted us. She pulled it up as she checked her messages. "Damn, I just lost a long-term tenant at our beach duplex in Myrtle Beach. You don't know of anyone who wants to rent a place for a week or even the entire summer, do you?"

"I don't know of anyone off the top of my mind. I'll keep my eyes open, though."

"Thank you, Chip. You have my number if anyone comes to mind, or for any other reason." She blew me a kiss and walked around the back of the SUV toward the school entrance.

The bell rang, and within a minute, the doors burst open with happy middle schoolers rushing out to begin their summer vacation. I walked to the entrance and waited patiently for a lag in the flow of kids so I could enter. Sadie told me I could meet her at the art studio. I signed in with the guard by the door and slapped on my sticky visitor badge.

The crowds of enthusiastic students thinned out. I walked down the stairs to the lower level, where the art studio was located. Mrs. Phelps, the art teacher, waited with Sadie and a few other students who were picking up their projects.

Sadie waited by a rolling media cart loaded with her various sculptures and painted display items. "Hi, Uncle Chip. I loaded up all my things. Mrs. Phelps said she can unlock the elevator and we can go up to the first floor that way."

"Would it make more sense for me to drive the truck around back and we can go right out the doors on this level?"

The teacher came over. "Hi, Mr. Proctor. Yes, that will be easier. Otherwise, I have to ring the custodian to run the elevator."

"Great, I'll be right back. Sadie, bring your cart down to the rear double doors."

Mrs. Phelps said, "Do you need me to come out and wave so you know which entrance it is?"

"No, I know where the double doors are. Right across from the athletic fields." I smiled a thank you and glanced over at Sadie. "I'll be right there. Wait for me inside the doors, okay?"

"Okay."

I went back out front to my SUV and drove around the building to the rear of the school, making a wide circle around a group of kids next to the small skateboard park attached to the athletic fields.

Sadie opened the doors when I pulled up and wheeled out the cart with her art projects. It took a few minutes to load them in the back. When we finished, I lowered the hatch.

"Sadie, hon, take the cart back inside to Mrs. Phelps." I turned and bumped into the unattended cart. Sadie wasn't with it.

I looked around and spotted her halfway across the parking lot. She stared over at the kids by the skate park, her arms stiff at her sides and her hands clenched.

An icy chill stung my chest. I touched my gold shark's tooth necklace, which had been a gift from my dead brother. It pulsed with freezing power, a sign only activated when it protected me from powerful magic nearby. There was a threat close, and that put Sadie in danger.

My hand dropped to the six-inch leather-wrapped cylinder clipped to my belt. I never went anywhere without my Guardian weapon. I didn't want to deploy the magical sword just yet. It was best to keep it hidden until I identified the threat.

A visual search of the area revealed nothing I could see. The only people in view were the stationary Sadie and the kids with their skateboards across the parking lot.

"Sadie, come here. There's something wrong." I reached toward her. "Come on back to the truck, hon. We need to go. Now."

She remained there, her attention locked on the kids.

The hair on my arms stood at attention. Magical energy crackled around me. Whatever was coming was close.

I craned my neck, searching all around us. Nothing leaped out at me as dangerous. I rushed over to Sadie. When I stopped beside her, the goosebumps on my closest arm went all the way to eleven. A shiver passed up that side of my body.

I rubbed at the chill coursing up my arm. The icy cold of my shark's tooth amulet had grown even sharper, as if it were burning my skin. "Sadie, come on. It's time to leave."

She didn't respond. The air around her shimmered with power, like the waves of heat coming off summer asphalt. The effect extended several inches around her entire body. Tears streamed down her face as she stared at the group of kids over by the skate park.

Had she identified a threat I couldn't see?

I scanned the park to see what or who she looked at. Then I spotted Patty Peyton and her daughter, Astrid. Astrid stood next to a tall, blond boy with shoulder-length hair and a skateboard leaning up against his leg.

Astrid gazed up at the boy and twirled her long, blonde locks around one finger. With her other hand, she pointed at the halfpipe.

The boy nodded and climbed the steps at the rear of the half-pipe. He set his skateboard down at the top of the halfpipe and waved at Astrid. Then he jumped on the board and rode it down one side, across the bottom, and up the far side where he leaped up into the air.

Beside me, Sadie sobbed and let out the faintest of whispers, "Why?"

I felt, rather than saw, the wave of power blasting away from her toward the skate park. It didn't even occur to me to shout a warning.

A second later, the board flipped away from the boy's feet right before he came down to descend the halfpipe again. His leg hit the edge.

Even across the parking lot, I imagined I heard the crack as the bone broke.

Sadie's hands came up to her face. Horror filled her eyes. The tears flowed even faster. She whirled around and raced to the passenger side of the SUV. Her hands worked to lift the handle, but the door was still locked.

I looked back over at the skate park. Everyone had clustered around the collapsed kid.

Everyone except Patty Peyton. Her brows lowered as she stared in my direction. Then she pulled out her phone and returned her attention to the circle of kids around the injured skater.

Back at the SUV, Sadie waited until I returned. I unlocked the passenger door with my key fob. She jumped into the front seat.

I pushed the empty media cart over to the open double doors. I didn't want to leave Sadie alone outside, so I didn't return it all the way to Mrs. Phelps. I left it in the hallway and returned to my vehicle.

I climbed into the driver's seat.

Before I glanced her way, Sadie said, "We have to leave, Uncle Chip. We have to go. Now."

"Sadie, honey, what happened back there?"

"I-I-I don't know." She twisted in her seatbelt to face me. Her face screwed up in pain, and tears streamed down her cheeks. "I didn't mean to hurt him. I swear."

"You did that?"

"I don't know. I didn't mean for anything bad to happen. Maybe?"

"Okay, but we should talk about this. Has this happened before?"

Sadie went rigid as if trying to control something inside. "I don't think so. We have to go home. Please, before anyone sees me crying like this."

I shifted into drive and pulled away. A siren sounded in the distance. Patty must've called for an ambulance. I put on a smile and directed it at Sadie. "Aunt Rose will know what to do."

"I know. I have to call her, but not until we get home. This is awful." Her words choked out between sobs. "Please, Uncle Chip. Take me home."

There was nothing else to do. Patty was here, so there was an adult with the injured boy, and the authorities were on the way. There was no need to remain. My foot pressed down, and the SUV sped away from the action at the far end of the lot. I wasn't sure what had happened back there, but it seemed Sadie had something to do with it. It was clear she thought so, too.

If the threat I'd detected had come from her somehow, I needed to understand it. I was supposed to protect her, not protect people from her. This added a whole new wrinkle to being her Guardian. Once again, things in the family had become all too confusing.

We drove home in silence. My mind spun through the possibilities based on my limited knowledge of Fae magic and what little Fae girls could do with it. The only thing I could think of was we needed to call Rose and figure out what had happened right away. I hoped my parenting counterpart would know the answer to what I'd just witnessed.

5

Rose

I groaned when my fourth alarm went off. My hand fumbled over the nightstand before I remembered throwing my phone on the floor after shutting off the third alarm I'd set the night before.

Ugh.

I rolled to the edge of the bed and peered out through slitted eyes at the phone blaring music at me from the floor. ACDC's *Back in Black* was a great song, but not for people with lingering jet lag.

My arm stretched toward it but was six inches too short. I was going to have to actually sit up and get out of bed this time. It was probably a sign from above to awaken and take on the new day. I squinted at the clock on the nightstand. It was approaching mid-afternoon.

There were things to do. I hoped to get everything finished and still have time to surprise Chip and the kids to let them know I'd returned from my trip. Business first, though.

It took two tries to sit up. The song had moved well into the second chorus by the time my feet made it to the floor, and I stretched forward to shut it off. Part of the reason for my fatigue was I hadn't fully restored my mana since expending so much of it in Scotland two days before. I needed to eat some real, non-airline food and prop up my mind with more than a little caffeine.

While I had my phone in my hand, I checked my messages. I'd sent one to Warren last night before I hit the sack. He'd responded, telling me he couldn't meet until after seven tonight. The response irked me a little. I was his primary client, after all. He was on a retainer with the family to keep up the investigation into the accident nine years before. Plus, he had other duties searching out the subsequent queries and incursions sent to track down Sadie.

I looked away from the phone. I wouldn't get anywhere being angry at Warren, so I shifted gears to my other task for the afternoon. I had to track down Hitch and see if I could get him to conjure up some more powerful masking magic for Chip and the kids. The trick would be to get him to do it without giving up Sadie's identity as the future Fae Queen. I trusted the freelance wizard far less than the distance I could throw him. He was the poster boy for wizard mercenary, and he'd sell anything he knew to the right buyer. It would be a pain to hide the body if he discovered the truth about my niece.

I'd tried texting him the night before, hoping he'd actually respond to my request to meet up. As usual, he ghosted me. It was no use trying to call him either. He wouldn't pick up when he hadn't respond to my texts.

Luckily, before I left the country, Warren had texted me Hitch's current flop-house apartment address. I'd pay him a visit in person. Then he couldn't weasel out of working for me. It wasn't like I'd threatened him every time we'd worked together. Just most of them.

I pulled on my jeans and slipped into a black tank top. I stared across the apartment at the small kitchen and the coffee machine. That was too much work. I decided to hit up Dunkin' for coffee on the way to Hitch's place instead. I could grab a bagel sandwich there, too, which would boost up my mana better than just coffee. There wasn't any food worth eating in my cabinets or fridge. My solitary bachelorette lifestyle didn't lend itself to keeping a full pantry.

The egg and bacon sandwich was a good choice. I felt far more alive and energized once I'd finished it and half of the iced latte. I parked on the street out in front of the apartment building where

Warren had said Hitch lived. Not surprisingly, it was a dump. I wondered what such a talented wizard spent all his spell money on to end up in places like this. Warren had once said it was bad choices in women and wagers. It made sense. Both had a way of being bad news.

I took one more sip of my drink and got out of the Firebird. Time to wake up the wizard and make him pay for not returning my texts. I made it halfway to the door when I heard shouting upstairs. Someone was getting a pretty good beating, judging from the wailing echoing out onto the sidewalk below.

I shook my head. It wasn't my problem. *Eyes forward, Rose. You're just here to see Hitch.*

Up on the second floor, I ignored the sounds of struggle coming from the one open apartment door. I searched for apartment F. There was apartment D, E, open door, and finally G.

Damn. What had Hitch gotten himself into this time?

I walked over to the open door but didn't enter. I could see plenty from the entrance.

A massive hand pressed the wheezing wizard up against the far wall, the fingers pressing in around his throat. Another hand cocked back to take a swing at his swollen face. Both hands belonged to a hairy brute with the distinct odor of boar. Hitch had gotten on the wrong side of another angry shifter.

I considered turning around and leaving him to his trouble. There were other spell casters I could reach out to.

Hitch's eyes locked onto mine. He croaked, "R-R-Rose, please. M-m-make him stop."

The wereboar turned his head and leered over his shoulder at me. "Get outa here, wench. This isn't your fight."

I thought about the shifter's words for a second or two. Even slurred by his upthrust tusks, I understood him well enough.

"Rose." Hitch sucked in another breath. "Please."

Hitch's wheezy call for help aside, it was being called a wench that tipped the balance for me. Who even did that anymore?

"Put the wizard down."

The boar's eyes narrowed. "Are you serious? A skinny little thing like you thinks she can take me down?"

"Thanks for calling me skinny, but yeah. I kind of need to talk to him, and I'm afraid you're going to kill him by accident. That would be an inconvenience I don't need right now."

The cocked fist rocketed forward, hitting Hitch in the side of his face. His eyes rolled up in his head, and his struggling body went limp.

For a second, I worried he was dead, but he groaned when the wereboar let go of him and he slumped to the floor.

The goon turned around and pounded his fist into his hand. "I don't usually beat up on the ladies. Maybe you'd like to take it out in trade?"

The leer on his face left no question of where his thoughts were going.

"Or you could leave now, while you still have enough manhood dangling between your legs to procreate."

The boar snarled his response and charged at me. I didn't have any silver on me, and I'd left my sword in the car, but I had more than enough gas in the tank after my recent meal to take out this lone shifter.

Right before his outstretched hands reached me, I spun away from the open doorway.

The surprised shifter tried to slow down his charge and skidded out into the hallway. He barely stopped before he toppled over the stair railing down to the first floor.

My spinning twist finished in a well-timed roundhouse kick to the side of the wereboar's head.

His head swung around, spittle flying from his open mouth. He stumbled a few feet down the hallway with his hands to his face.

When he turned around to face me, he held out a hand. A large tusk lay in his palm. "You broke my toof."

"You're a shifter. It'll grow back."

The snarling growl betrayed the charge that followed.

I ducked low, my leg striking out and kicking his leading knee at the moment his weight came down on it. The joint buckled inward, and the wereboar bellowed in pain. He dropped to the floor, clutching at his leg with both hands, the broken tooth falling to the floor beside him.

I didn't have time to play anymore. I stepped over the curled-up beast and leveled a snap kick to the back of his head.

This time, it was his turn to get knocked out. His body went limp, and he reverted to his usual human form. The man that lay there had the body of an accountant, not the bruiser I'd expected.

Edging around the wall, I entered the apartment and closed the door. Just in case the goon on the other side woke up before I was finished with my business, I locked the deadbolt and drew on my limited mana to strengthen the wooden doorframe. That would hold the guy should he decide to enter again.

By the time I was finished with the door, Hitch had pushed himself up to a seated position with his back against the far wall.

"Wow, Rose, am I ever glad to see you."

"You wouldn't know it from the way you ghosted me after I texted you last night."

Hitch climbed to his feet and steadied his wobbly body by leaning on the kitchen table. "If I'd answered you, then you wouldn't be here now, would you?"

I laughed. "Nice try, Hitch, but precognition isn't your thing. You were avoiding me."

"Fair enough. But I knew if it was important enough, you'd come and find me. And here you are. What's the special magic you need this time? You finally want me to mix up a love charm for you to use on that Chip guy?"

"Ewww, no," I said. "If I ever want to close that deal, I can do it on my own."

Hitch held up both hands. "Methinks you doth protest too much. I've seen the way you two look at each other when you think the other one's not watching. I say do the deed and get it over with."

"I'm not here to talk about my love life. I certainly don't want one of your sketchy love charms."

"Okay, what are you here for, then?" Hitch pulled out one of the two plastic kitchen chairs and sat down. He gestured for me to take the other one.

I realized we'd reached the negotiation part of the discussion and sat down opposite the wizard. "I need to know what you can do to mask wild magic."

"Why, has there been an outbreak again? I've felt a few rumblings lately, but they're over before I can localize the source. If there's someone dabbling out there, we should stop them, not try to mask what they're doing."

It took me a second before I latched on to what he said. "You've felt someone using wild magic? Why didn't you tell me that? When?" If Hitch had detected it, it could be what the warlock in Scotland referred to.

"I dunno. The first was a few months back. It happened so quick, I assumed I imagined it. Ya know?"

"What about the other times?" I needed to know what he knew.

"The next few times were stronger and lasted longer. Each time was about a month after the time before. I guess there've been four in all. The last was a few weeks ago."

"All right. I know you don't think it's a good idea, but if you could mask the source, how would you do it?"

Hitch's face screwed up in thought, and he tilted his head up at the water-stained plaster ceiling above. "I'm not sure I could. Given how strong it would have to be to be felt at any distance, it would probably burn right through anything I cast to cover or contain it. If you needed to hide it, you'd be better off going to a natural source of wild magic and using its emanations as a distraction from the releases."

I started to ask him for a better explanation when his eyes widened, and he slammed his fist down on the table. His other hand rubbed at his forehead. "There, there it is again. Can you feel it? It's throbbing with even more power this time. Agh, it's like the worst sinus headache ever."

I did sense a sort of throbbing at the back of my mind. If Hitch hadn't pointed it out to me, I might have dismissed it as an early migraine. My eyes shifted as my face turned to the west. Whatever it was, it lay in that direction. What was over there?

Then I realized the magical sensation had a tinge of familiarity. Sadie's school lay in that direction less than a mile away.

Hitch pointed at me. "You felt it. See, I told you. It's way more powerful than anything I could hide."

"I have to go." I stood, canceled my spell on the entrance, and unlocked the door. As it swung open, I stepped over the still unconscious shifter in the hallway. "I suggest you get lost before the wereboar wakes up. Tell Warren where you end up. I'll have some work for you soon. Don't make me come looking for you again."

"Sure, Rose. Whatever you say. I told you it was powerful. Are you going to hunt the guy down? Messing with wild magic is just plain stupid."

"You let me deal with it. Forget we talked about this. I mean it. If I hear you've been gabbing around town about me and this wild magic thing, I'll come and finish the job our piggy friend here started."

"Yeah, I know how to keep my mouth shut. See ya, Rose. Don't be a stranger."

I huffed and stomped down the stairs. My phone was out before I was halfway to the car. I sent off a quick text to Chip.

Where RU?

He didn't answer. I headed for the house. Today was the last day of school, and the kids were already dismissed. Whatever had happened, I hoped Sadie was already on the way home and nowhere near the wild magic outbreak. Of course, in my soul, I knew that hope was wrong.

6

Chip

I had barely backed into the garage before Sadie jumped out and ran in through the door to the kitchen. I shifted into park and turned off the SUV. Across the street, Addy played with Ellie's youngest and another neighborhood kid in the front yard. The other mom had gotten him off the elementary school bus just like I'd asked.

When he saw me wave from the open garage door, he waved back and went on playing with his friends. I left the door up for him when he came home and went inside. Ellie would send him over before dinnertime once she saw my SUV parked inside. It was part of the neighborhood shorthand between the parents in the cluster at the end of the street.

Having Addy playing elsewhere would make it easier to talk to Sadie about what had happened at the middle school. Addy always wanted to take part in the family discussions about their royal lineage and his sister's place in it. He envisioned himself as a great Fae warrior someday. I smiled. He had the athleticism for it, gaining the genes from both sides of the family. Rose said he had a decent capability for magic, too. Hopefully, it didn't bubble up to the surface someday the way Sadie's powers had today.

I fished in my pocket for my phone. I saw a text from Rose.

Where RU?

She was at the top of my favorite contacts, so I started a call to her. She beat me to it, though, and I picked up right away.

"Hey, Rose, I'm glad you called—"

"Chip, what happened with Sadie? Is she all right? There was an immense surge of wild magic from the direction of the middle school. Tell me it wasn't her."

"She's okay," I began. "Wait, you felt that?"

"You bet I did. So did anyone with magical sensitivity within a few miles of it, maybe even farther." She paused. "Where are you?"

"We're home. Sadie ran up to her room. She didn't talk about it all the way home."

"Good," Rose replied. "I'm almost there. Make sure she doesn't do anything else like what happened earlier."

Recalling the boy who was involved, I said, "I don't think she'll do it again."

"What makes you so sure?"

"Because the cause of it is far away from here, probably on the way to the hospital."

"Hospital! You mean people saw what happened?" She muttered something I couldn't hear, then said, "Never mind. I'm pulling in now. This is worse than I thought."

The line went dead. I shook my head. I'd admit, what had happened was something to be concerned about, but Rose had a way of making everything into the end of the world. I left Sadie alone up in her room and waited for Rose to come in.

A few seconds later, the door to the garage burst open, and my sister-in-law strode into the kitchen. "Is she still upstairs?" Rose headed toward the steps.

"Yes, but Rose, stop." I moved in front of her. "Tell me what happened out there. One second we were loading up some of Sadie's artwork, and the next thing there was this power everywhere. I felt it all over. It lifted the hairs on my neck and arms."

Rose put her hands on her hips, and for a second, I thought she was going to push past me. Then she shrugged. "I guess it's over for now. That thing you felt was a surge of wild magic. There's always some sort of manifestation whenever a high-Fae child reaches this age. It's usually weak and isolated to a few odd occurrences here and there."

I scowled and tried to understand. "What kind of odd occurrences are we talking about here, Rose? What I witnessed surpassed 'odd' by far."

"When I was growing up, my wild magic surfaced by causing every insect and creepy-crawly thing within twenty feet to emerge and try to get as far away from me as possible. It only happened five or six times before I learned to control it. Lili had a short period where every flowering plant near her burst into full bloom, even if it had been dead. It was so typical for Lili to manifest beauty wherever she went, while I was the bug queen."

"So, Sadie can control it? That's good."

"Maybe not," Rose said. "Even with the relatively minor surges Lili and I had, it took us several weeks to learn to sense and tamp them down before they surfaced. What Sadie is doing is a hundred times more powerful, and it's attracting attention from the very forces we've been afraid would find her."

"Then you and Allura have to teach her to get it under control faster. You're the magic experts in the family. We can't have that kind of thing happen again."

Rose frowned. "It's not that easy. This is the old magic—the Queen's powers—rising to the surface. This is something Sadie has to wrestle with. The best we can do is to try to mask it until she grows into being able to control it."

Sadie had walked in to stand in the kitchen doorway. "How long will that take, Aunt Rose? I mean, I can't be some kind of freak all summer long."

I stepped to the side as Rose held out her arms. Sadie rushed into her aunt's embrace. Tears streamed down her cheeks and dripped onto the shoulder of Rose's worn leather jacket. When had our girl gotten so tall?

I patted Sadie's back. "It'll be okay, kiddo. Your aunt and I have got this covered."

Sadie stepped back to look at the two of us. "What does that mean? I don't know why all this is happening. It just blows up from inside me. Where is it coming from?"

Rose said, "It's from the well of wild magic the Queen of the Fae is destined to control. The ability to access it is hidden within all Fae, but the royal family and the Queen's line in particular have a special connection with it."

"If you can touch it, too, then tell me how to control it."

"I have tried to teach you to be exact in your spells and magic," Rose started. "I hoped that would give you the rigid structure that would help you contain some of this. It appears I was wrong. We'll have to try something else."

"Wrong? I hurt someone today, and you want to *try* something? I'm turning into a monster, and you're experimenting with me." Sadie threw her hands in the air, spun around, and stalked over to look out the sliding door into the fenced-in backyard. "I guess I'll just hide out here in the house and yard all summer. I can't afford to be around any of my friends with this going on. I might hurt someone else."

I looked at Rose and then back at Sadie. "Rose and I will come up with something to help you get a handle on this, Sadie. We'll have it under control before you know it."

"Maybe not," Rose said. "Sadie is just past her thirteenth birthday. My guess is, the outbreaks are going to grow in strength, at least for a little while."

Sadie swiveled around to face us. "This is going to get worse?" She crossed her arms. "You have to do something. You're the adults here. Fix this."

"It's not that simple," Rose said. "Plus, there are other concerns that we have to worry about on top of it."

"More than me blowing up again and hurting someone?"

Rose nodded. "These wild magic surges are drawing attention to the area from people sensitive to wild magic outbreaks. That includes people who have been looking for the Queen's power to manifest."

She'd mentioned this earlier. "Rose, what does that mean? Should we expect trouble here at the house? It's been so long since anyone attacked us here, I thought we'd been able to keep this place a secret."

"It still is, for now. I just got back from Scotland. I was tracking down a lead Warren turned up. It linked back to Lili and Bobby's incident."

Sadie said, "You mean when someone killed them? If the person responsible for that comes around, maybe I can channel some of this power into hurting them."

"No," Rose and I said in tandem.

Rose continued. "It's too early for you to try to control the power coming from inside you. You'd be just as likely to hurt an innocent bystander as your target. Besides, this one is strong, stronger than me. And they've sensed the rising wild magic and located it to somewhere on America's east coast. They're going to try to home in on the location here before the outbreaks stop. We can't let that happen."

"You just told us this person was stronger than you," I said. "If they're that dangerous, we have to come up with a plan to keep them from finding us."

"That's what Allura and I have planned. We have to go where there's so much wild magic in the background that your surges won't stand out." Rose smiled at Sadie. "That's a place we can learn to control and direct the magic."

Sadie said, "Okay, where do we go? I wanted to play soccer in the travel league this summer, but I can't be around my friends with this happening."

"No, you can't," I said. "Someone else will get hurt for sure, and people will notice. Miss Patty already suspects something."

Rose's eyes went wide. "Patty saw what happened today?"

"Yeah," I said. "She and Astrid were near the skate park where the boy was injured. When we left, Patty was watching our SUV leave the school lot."

"That's not good, Chip."

"Look, Rose. I know Patty isn't your favorite person, but she wouldn't do anything to hurt Sadie or any of us."

Rose snorted a laugh. "That's not your brain talking there, Chip. If Patty even suspects who Sadie is, she won't keep her mouth shut. She'll let it slip to the other Fae nobles. They'll all want to curry favor to get close to the future queen. We can't have that. Not yet."

The doorbell rang.

Sadie said, "I'll get it. You two figure out where we need to go to keep me from hurting any more of my friends." She left Rose and me in the kitchen, staring at each other, annoyed as usual.

After Sadie left, I said, "Rose, you need to let this thing against Patty go. She's not the mean girl who bothered you in high school. Besides, it's not like we're going out anymore. You did your best to make that so awkward that she got the hint. I don't think she has eyes on me like that now."

"All the single moms have eyes for you. That's what makes you so infuriating all the time. You act like you're oblivious to it, but we both know that's not true."

"So what if they do? Are you annoyed because you missed your turn and want another shot at the old Chipster?"

I regretted it as soon as the words left my mouth. It wasn't because they weren't true, maybe. It was because of the instant hurt in Rose's eyes and the way her spine stiffened. She'd become my partner in raising both the kids. We were a team, and you didn't hurt your teammates.

I opened my mouth to say I was sorry when a roaring snarl echoed into the house from the front door. Sadie's battle cry followed it, along with a shout of "Aunt Rose, to arms!"

7

Rose

Sadie's war cry awakened the inner arms-mistress in me. Reaching to my back, I cursed. My sword was out in my car and of little use to me now.

Chip's hand went to his belt. His collapsable magic sword hilt came away in his fingers, and in a flash, the meter of enchanted steel extended out. He dashed from the room toward the ring of clashing metal in the front hall.

Without my weapon of choice, I raced after him, grabbing the large and small chef's knives on my way past the butcher block knife holder on the counter.

I ran through the dining room and around the foot of the stairs to the front room and foyer.

Sadie held a cutlass from the ornamental display on the wall. In this home, no weapon was purely decorative, and the future Fae queen displayed the hours of practice she'd put in over the years.

She fended off a dark, humanoid creature wearing the plain brown shorts and button-down shirt of the regular delivery truck driver. Since that driver wasn't an undead shade, this attacker had either killed him for his uniform or stolen one just like it.

The dark shade had a dagger. The foot-long blade dripped a

glowing green goo onto the carpeted floor. Each drop left a dark spot and a wisp of smoke where it fell.

"Don't let him touch you, Sadie. That dagger is poisoned."

Despite the seriousness of the situation, she still rolled her eyes and glared at me. "You think?"

The shade, its human form faded to a translucent, cloudy gray outline of a person, saw an opportunity when Sadie broke her concentration. It lunged at her midsection with the dagger.

Chip dove forward, somehow covering the distance between himself and the struggling pair by the door. His outstretched sword batted the dagger away so it missed Sadie's side by mere inches.

Now that Chip and I had arrived, the Shade would probably try to escape. There was no way he could take all three of us.

The shade arrived at a completely different conclusion. The creature darted backward to the open doorway. It let out a screeching howl, and its form blurred as if vibrating in place.

A second later, two identical shades separated from the center one in the brown shorts and shirt. The shadow forms split away, and two came directly at me and Chip. The original attacker returned to its first target, Sadie.

In the brief break, Sadie had grabbed the metal buckler from the display where she'd gotten the cutlass. The dinner-plate-sized shield wouldn't be much help, but at least it gave her some additional defense against the foul blade wielded against her.

There was no time to focus on Sadie. We had attackers of our own to deal with.

Chip kept his shade at bay to one side with his glowing Guardian's sword. The magical blade could pierce even the shadow form with its enchantments, and the shade appeared to realize it, keeping a little distance.

I, on the other hand, didn't have magical weapons. My shade leaped at me. I stabbed at it with both knives. They both passed through the shade's non corporeal form, doing no noticeable damage. They were forged from cold iron, not stainless steel, so they might have had some effect. Judging from the lack of reaction, though, that wasn't enough to keep it at bay.

The moaning creature wrapped its arms around me. I could barely feel the shade's physical embrace, but the icy cold penetrating the depths of my being left no doubt it was affecting me. Shades could sap the life force from a living being. If I did nothing, it would suck all my energy as it fed.

However, I wasn't without my own powers. I called up my recently restored mana stores and drew the energy into a blazing ball of life-force. The powerful spell manifested as a sphere of blinding light in my fist.

I punched forward, burying my fist in the shade's head.

The shadow's mouth opened, and a howl of pain escaped. It let go of its embrace and tried to pull back.

"Not so easy when someone fights back, is it?" I shouted. I lunged after it, keeping my hand buried in its shadowy skull.

Initially, the light had dimmed as it passed through the creature's outer layers. Now it grew in brilliance as it consumed the shade's dark form from the inside out.

The shade's very solid hands with cracked and blackened skin reached up to grip my wrist where it entered the creature's head. It tugged at my arm with its icy grip, trying to dislodge me from my attack.

I wouldn't be denied. They didn't get to come in here, in this place, and attack my family.

I drew in more energy and fed it to the ball of force in my hand. The howling increased in volume until it almost deafened me. I had to end this.

My clenched fingers were visible now through the faint outline of the shade's fading form. I twisted my wrist, trying to find that one spot that was the shade's core so I could end the undead being.

The shade's clutching hands stiffened and then shot out as the creature spread-eagled in midair, centered on my extended hand and my ball of power.

Then, after vibrating where it hung for a few long seconds, the shade winked out of existence with a soft pop. I gasped from the energy expenditure, and my hand dropped to my side.

By the door, Sadie chopped down at the lunging delivery-man

shade with her cutlass. Unlike my kitchen knives, the cutlass was Fae forged and not the ornamental piece everyone assumed it was.

The broad blade flashed bright blue as my niece fed it power. She cut through the forearm holding the deadly dagger, and the shadow's hand disappeared. The weapon dropped to the carpet.

"Keep up the attack. It can reform itself if given the chance." I hoped my shouted instructions wouldn't be met with another snarky eyeroll.

Luckily for Sadie, she didn't waste the energy. Maybe she'd learned her lesson about giving in to teen snark in the middle of combat. Sadie twisted in place, pivoting perfectly on the ball of her right foot.

She extended her arm. The cutlass blade swept around in a broad circle. The shade let out a piercing cry, cut short when the Fae-forged cold steel cut through its shadowy neck.

For an instant, the head hovered an inch above the collapsing body, then both head and body popped out of existence like the one I'd dispatched. The brown delivery shirt and shorts dropped to the floor in a heap.

Two down and one left.

I turned my attention to give Chip some help.

Chip stood with one hand extended, palm out. He used his invisible barrier ability to press the final shade against the wall beside the large bay window. He kept his Guardian sword level at his waist, ready to lunge at the shade.

Sadie snarled and let out her war cry. Before I could stop her, she leaped at the final enemy and slashed down from above with her cutlass. Her sapphire eyes flashed, and blue fire rippled along the blade.

The descending sword cut down, cleaving the shade's forehead open all the way down to where its navel would have been if it had been a living creature.

Both Chip and I shouted, "No!"

The shade's two parting halves split, then the creature popped out of existence like the other two.

"Sadie," I said. "We could have questioned it."

She frowned and said, "Why? They're undead minions sent by a necromancer or sorcerer. They're not going to tell us anything."

Chip said, "Your aunt is right. You don't know that for sure. I was hoping we could somehow use them to identify the summoner."

I swallowed a snarky comment about Chip finally learning something about the more obscure creatures and magical beings. "What's done is done. Chip, check outside, then close the front door. We don't need the neighbors coming by to check on the noises from our attackers."

He walked to the front door and stopped. "Uh, what do we do about the brown delivery truck outside? It's sitting there by the driveway."

"Damn," I replied. "Let me call Warren. He can bring someone to take it away before people start asking questions. I'll bet there's a body in the back who used to wear that uniform." I stared down at the pile of clothes on the floor.

I pulled out my phone and sent a quick text message to the werewolf.

As I did, Chip closed the front door. "What do we do with the poisoned dagger?"

The dagger had fallen on the carpet, or what used to be the carpet. A six-inch section had dissolved from the dripping blade's poison.

"Stay away from it. I'll dispose of it. It'll need to be cleansed first, and that'll take a favor from Hitch." I wasn't looking forward to owing the warlock anything, but I couldn't risk that dagger getting found by some unsuspecting kid. That poison seemed more like the demonic possession kind than the killing kind.

The front door opened, and Addy froze, staring down at the dagger. "Awesome! Where'd that come from? Can I have it?"

"No," Chip said. "Aunt Rose was just about to deal with it. Come in and close the door."

I bent down and picked up the dagger. The poison had mostly dripped away, leaving a sticky, pale-green coating on the blade itself. I held it down at my side, careful to keep it away from me and the others.

Addy closed the door. "Hey, there's an empty delivery truck parked out front. Weird."

"We saw it," I said. "You were over at Miss Ellie's playing. Did anyone comment about the truck?"

"Nope. I only saw it because I had to walk past it while coming home for dinner."

I hoped Warren hurried up getting someone to retrieve it. It wouldn't go unnoticed here at the back end of the street for long.

"Chip, I need to dispose of this and make sure Warren follows up with the truck." Recalling my conversation with Aunt Allura, I added, "Figure out somewhere for us all to go for a while. It would be better if it was near a lot of natural energy to mask the wild magic. Try the area around Myrtle Beach, South Carolina, if you can." Now he'd think it was his idea.

Sadie frowned. "This is because of me. Maybe I should just run away."

I ignored the teen drama coming from my niece.

Chip said, "Myrtle Beach is a good choice. Should we get a house for the entire summer?"

"Yes, that would be perfect. Myrtle Beach is close to the Gulf Stream. We can kill two birds with one stone down there."

Chip concentrated on his sword for a second. The blade disappeared down into the hilt. "I think I know of a place there. Hopefully, it's still available. I'll get on it." He clipped the hilt back onto his belt. "Wait, what did you mean by killing two birds on this trip?"

"Just another opportunity to secure Sadie's future." I dropped it. He didn't need to know more until I had set up some things. "When you have a place, let me know. I'll meet you there. Don't wait for me. Pack up the kids and leave. Don't tell anyone else where you're going."

"Of course. I know how to keep a secret."

I glared at him to let him know what I thought of that statement. We both knew his history on that count. I headed for the car. The big brown delivery van had pulled up behind where I'd parked the Firebird. I pulled out my phone, took a deep breath, and tapped to call Hitch. I wasn't in the mood for the warlock's drama, but this was urgent. While I handled that, I'd have to trust Chip to take care of things here at home.

Chip

It took us over an hour to pack up the SUV for the trip to the beach, and it was almost dinnertime before we were ready to go. "Addy, double check and make sure you packed your swim trunks."

"I packed them, Uncle Chip. I swear."

"Just check again." I pulled out my phone. I needed to make a call, and I didn't want the kids to overhear who I was talking to. I was worried Patty might have questions about the events earlier in the afternoon.

The connection rang a few times before Patty picked up. "Chip, I was thinking of calling you. Did Sadie say anything to you about sensing something unusual in the magical spectrum this afternoon?"

"Um, no, not really. She was her usual quiet teen self. You know how it is, buried in her phone the whole ride home. Why do you ask?" I hoped I had put her off the scent.

"No reason, I guess. Something weird happened at the school earlier. Anyway, why did you call? Were you looking for a dinner date?"

"Actually, I was checking to see if that place down in Myrtle Beach was still open. I decided to take the kids on a trip for the summer. How many bedrooms does it have? If it's big enough, I'll take it all the way until school starts again."

"The whole summer?" Patty asked. "I haven't even told you how much it is to rent."

"You're not going to jack up the prices on me, are you?"

She laughed. "No, of course not. It has four bedrooms including a master suite on the first floor. Plus, you're in luck. I've only had a few nibbles since I talked with you. There's nothing concrete yet, and if you'll take it all summer, I'll cancel the appointments I have scheduled so far."

"Great. Email me the documents for the lease. Any chance we can check in tonight?"

"It's eight hours from here, Chip. You won't get there until after midnight."

"I'm trying to be spontaneous and surprise the kids. It's hard to get them excited about anything at this age. I thought a last-minute trip to the beach for vacation would break through the angst."

"Astrid has been unbearable lately, so I know what you mean." Patty's voice changed on the other end. "I put you on speaker so I can look up the realtor's address and email on my laptop. I'll contact them, and they'll take care of the details. They have a coded lock box at their office where you can pick up the keys no matter what time you arrive."

Addy came down with his swim trunks in hand. He hadn't packed them after all. I waved him over to put them in his suitcase. "Great. I'll watch for the email to pick up the keys and get the address. Thanks for getting this arranged on the fly. I owe you one."

"Ooh, a favor from Chip?" Patty crooned over the phone. "I will definitely make time to collect on that. Don't forget now."

"Never. Thanks again."

Sadie walked into the living room, pulling her suitcase on its wheels behind her. She had a stuffed soccer backpack slung from her shoulders, too. "Who was that?"

"The person we're renting the summer place from. I had to arrange to pick up the keys late at night." I slid my phone into my jeans and smiled. "We're all set to make the trip down to Myrtle Beach."

"Never heard of it," Sadie said. "Is there anything fun to do there?"

"What?" I asked, resisting the urge to roll my eyes. "Besides the beach, the water, and everything that goes with an epic summer vacation?"

"Yeah, and none of my friends around to hang out with."

I didn't remind her it was her connection to some of her friends that was making us run away like this. "Come on. Let's load up and get on the road."

Addy groaned. "I'm hungry."

Nothing new there. He'd become a bottomless pit lately. "We'll pick up drive-thru on our way out of town."

"Really?"

"Yeah, really. Now load up." I waited for them to file by into the garage. I'd already loaded up all my stuff. Rose would see to having someone watch the house while we were gone. Knowing her, she'd be setting some traps for the next group of shades or whoever else showed up looking for the source of the magic surges.

We piled the last of the luggage into the SUV, and everybody buckled in. Sadie had called shotgun before Addy remembered, so she ended up in the front passenger seat. I hoped she was up for some conversation. She'd put her bare feet up on the dash and was already absorbed by her phone.

"You know the rule, Sadie."

"What?"

I backed out of the driveway. "Shotgun has to keep the driver awake. It's your job to chat me up or do something to keep me paying attention to the road."

"Fine, we can listen to one of my podcasts." She plugged in the cord coming from the center console's charging port. Her phone connected to the dashboard screen instantly. Within ten minutes, we were driving south listening to a pair of young women talking about K-dramas, accompanied by a dinner of fast-food cheeseburgers and shakes.

I shrugged. Neither of those were my first choices, but if giving them some options helped me connect with my noncommunicative charges, I would take it. I tried to pay attention to the podcast as I drove and got caught up on the discussion. It had picked up from the previous episode when Sadie started it.

We made great time. Eight and a half hours later, in the wee hours of the morning, I pulled up in front of a South Carolina real estate office. I reviewed the instructions in the email Patty had sent after I e-signed the summer lease. There was a metal box mounted on a post next to the parking lot. It had multiple doors with a small keypad and a screen on one side.

I got out of the SUV and tapped at the keypad with the box number and the four-digit code. One door popped open, and I grabbed the set of keys from inside before closing it. I waggled the keys in the air when I turned around so Sadie could see in the headlights. Addy was sound asleep in the back seat.

When I climbed in, Sadie said, "This is super sketchy, Uncle Chip. Anyone could come here and get those keys."

"Not unless they had the right code information. Besides, the keys were there, so no one else got them."

I entered the location of the rental property in my phone's GPS. It was ten minutes from the office. Sadie had her window down, despite the muggy air outside. She sniffed at the salty air, and a smile creased her face.

Making sure she didn't notice me watching her, I hid a small smile of my own. A lot had happened in the last twenty-four hours. Maybe a break in a seaside town was just what we needed.

The directions on the phone took me to a duplex house a block inland from the beach-front high-rise properties. I pulled into the single-car driveway beside our side of the home. We were closer to the water than I'd expected to be, within easy walking distance.

I got out and took a second to listen to the distant surf pounding on the beach. This was perfect. It didn't look like anyone was home in either unit. Patty hadn't mentioned it being two rental properties in one. Maybe she only owned half the house. Hopefully anyone staying next door were decent enough.

"Here we are, kiddos. Let's get loaded in, and then we can get some sleep. Sound good to you?"

Addy groaned from the back seat. "I was already asleep."

"Yeah, and once we're all loaded inside, you can find a real bed. Come on. Let's go check the place out."

Sadie had her backpack slung and her suitcase ready before I got Addy sufficiently awake to lend a hand.

I tossed her the keys. "Go unlock the front door and look around. Addy and I will bring in what we need right now. We can unload the rest in the morning."

Sadie caught the keyring and went to the front porch. A pair of wooden Adirondack chairs sat on the small porch, one on either side of the door. She opened it and went inside. I gave Addy his duffle bag and suitcase. Then I followed him with my suitcase, laptop bag, and backpack. The narrow three-story home looked perfect for us.

Sadie had already claimed the room on the top floor by the time I got inside. It was the smallest, but it had the perk of a ladder leading up to a hatch that opened onto a widow's walk on the roof. There were three other bedrooms, including one with bunk beds, a room with a double bed, and a master suite on the first floor with a queen bed and its own bathroom.

Since Rose would come down eventually, it was perfect. She could take the room with the double bed, and I'd settle into the master suite. That left Addy with the smaller room with the bunk beds to make his own.

"Settle in, gang. We're here for the whole summer."

"I feel like we're running away from something, Uncle Chip," Sadie said. "Shouldn't we stay and face what's coming after us?"

"Your Aunt Rose is correct on this one. You're not ready for what's out there looking for you yet. Let's get a handle on your power first. There'll be plenty of time before you're eighteen to confront anyone who comes along to attack us. In the meantime, that's what Aunt Rose and I are here for."

Addy said, "It'll be nice to have Aunt Rose staying with us. Will she be here all summer, too?"

"I think so, though I didn't ask her that outright." I hoped Rose was planning on staying. We needed her here to help navigate everything that was going on with Sadie. She had a better understanding of it than I ever would. First there was the female stuff. Add in all the Fae magic stuff, and I was way out of my league.

I pointed upstairs. "Get some sleep. I'm down here if you need me. I'll go shopping for some food in the morning, and then we can head out for a day on the beach."

Addy rubbed at his eyes and nodded. He was already half asleep again as he stumbled up the steps. Sadie followed him, dragging a little. I knew she had to be tired, but she'd stepped up and done her job keeping me awake on the drive. She'd earned her time in bed. I waited until I heard their doors close, then I went and checked the front and back entrances to make sure everything was locked up. It was time for me to sleep, too. Tomorrow would bring us the first day of summer break at the beach.

9

Rose

It took me two whole days to get things in place at home so I could head down to watch over Chip and the kids. I wasn't worried. They should be safe enough for a few days. Even Chip couldn't screw things up that quickly.

Hitch had way too many questions for me about why he was casting snooper spells on an empty house.

"Look, Rose. These kinds of spells are persnickety. They need a lot of TLC to keep them in tiptop shape."

"Hitch, you're not extorting me for more money. I already paid you for setting up the spells. You said you'd call me if anything tripped them while I was gone."

The greasy-haired warlock grinned, showing off a single gold tooth. That hadn't been there before, I was sure of it. I could guess what he had spent the advance payment on.

"Rose, I don't even know where you're going. How am I supposed to contact you about the spells if you don't tell me where to contact you?"

"That's not something you need to know. You have my number. Text or call if something happens."

"I still think I should get something. You pay Warren regularly. How about me, too?"

"You want a retainer?" I had my hands on my hips and glared at him.

"Uh, let's just call it a subscription. You know. Like the security monitoring services charge. That's what you're asking for. You wouldn't begrudge me that, at least."

"They charge fifty dollars a month. I suppose I could manage that."

"Yeah, but that's for a simple *mundane* security system. What you had me install is something much more complex."

I leaned forward onto the balls of my feet. "How complex?"

Hitch swallowed hard as he tried to match my gaze. "Call it $100 a week for the summer. You said your brother-in-law would be back before school starts up again."

I tallied up the cost and winced inside where Hitch couldn't see. I wouldn't give him the satisfaction. The fact was I needed him and his spells, and while he wasn't exactly trustworthy, I didn't think he'd double-cross me the way a total stranger would. If he said the spells needed upkeep, I'd have to take his word for it.

"Fine. I'll have my aunt set up regular cash payments to your account. That's all you're getting. If there's any more that needs doing, it comes out of your end."

The gold tooth gleamed when Hitch grinned again. "Deal. You won't be sorry. I'll keep the wards up to a hundred and ten percent all the time."

"See that you do. Warren will be watching you. If I find out you skipped town or disappeared on a bender, I will take it all back, along with giving you a beating, to remind you not to cross me. Got it?"

"Sure, Rose. I'd never do anything like that. Promise."

I nodded and left his apartment. I always felt like I needed a shower when I left his place. It was super skeevy.

Outside on Main Street, I climbed into my Firebird and revved the engine. I checked the time. I'd been up all night waiting for Hitch to return to his place. The sun was just peeking over the horizon. If I left now, I could be down in South Carolina by a little after lunch. I might even miss most of the traffic around Washington, D.C. by heading out this early.

I slipped the car into gear and pulled away to go south and join Chip and the kids. I didn't bother to text him that I was on the way. He'd be asleep. I'd message him when I stopped for gas and breakfast.

The long drive down Interstate 95 wore me down after no sleep the night before. By the time I drove into the outskirts of Myrtle Beach, I wasn't at my best. If I had been, my senses would have picked up on the line of motorcycles parked in front of the convenience store when I stopped for gas. Many motorcycle gangs had Unusual affiliations, and of those, many were of the more unsavory kind.

I got out of the Firebird and walked around to operate the gas pump. I rubbed at my eyes as the fuel filled my tank.

"Hey, hey, what do we have here?"

I didn't see the two hulking figures in biker leathers walk up behind me.

The second one sniffed the air. "Smells like there's some new Fae in town. Some mighty fine Fae at that."

I fight back the urge to roll my eyes at the ham-fisted pickup line. "Move along, guys. I'm tired and not in the mood to play right now." I hoped they'd take the hint and not press the issue.

"But we play real nice, girlie," the first guy said. "I haven't had a nice piece of Fae ass since I was in high school."

I inhaled and caught a scent of what kind of idiots we were working with here. Sea salt and rotting fish. Great, I'd stumbled into a gang of shark shifters. I snorted a laugh. "Who are you fooling? You never finished high school."

The second biker laughed. "Hey, she's right about that, Flick. You never graduated."

Another four gang members exited the store and moved around the parking lot so they could watch the fun play out. I didn't like the odds and looked around for some help. How come a cop never drove by when you needed one? I didn't want to kick off my arrival with a mass murder to explain. I had to figure a way out of this without killing anyone.

The first biker forced me to move when he started toward me with a hand outstretched to grab my arm.

I shifted my weight to my right foot and kicked out to the side with my left. The leather boot caught the first biker in the chest and sent him sprawling to the pavement behind my car. I whipped the gas nozzle from my tank and sprayed the fallen shifter with gasoline.

"Hey! What the hell, lady? I was just having some fun." He crabbed backward to get away from the puddle of volatile fuel.

His friend had moved over to help him, but I shook my head. I raised a forefinger, and a three-inch jet of flame rose from the end. "I'd stay where you are unless you have a burning desire to join your friend there." I raised the gas nozzle in his direction to punctuate my threat.

The largest member of the gang standing nearby took a step forward. "There's no need for that. This is just a misunderstanding. Flick's mouth gets him in trouble all the time. He didn't mean any harm."

This tall, muscular one must be the leader. I stared into his sea-foam blue eyes and held his gaze. "In that case, we can all go about our day with no further problems, right?" I raised one eyebrow and waited for the leader to answer. He was almost too attractive to be smart, too, but maybe he was the brains of the group as well as the brawn. There was always a first time.

"Jimbo, pick up Flick and come over here with us. I think the lady was just leaving."

"But, Fin, she can't get away with that, can she?" Jimbo asked without moving. "We run this town."

"Only because we don't upset the fish cart with the land folk. Think this through to its conclusion, and you'll see what I mean. Now do as I say. Now."

The unmistakable tone of an order hung in the air for just a second, then Jimbo helped the gasoline-soaked Flick to his feet, and they backed over to stand with the others.

I'd already swiped my card at the pump, so I didn't have to pay inside. I took two steps backward and returned the nozzle to the side of the pump. I made sure not to turn my back on the shifters as I returned to the driver's side and opened the door.

Before I got in, I gave a nod of acknowledgment to the leader, Fin. If this group of bozos really ran things around here, I would likely run into them again.

I left a ten-foot double strip of rubber as I pulled away onto the main road. When I was a few blocks away, I checked the rearview mirror. There were no bikes chasing after me, and I let out a sigh of relief.

I could've taken the first two idiots without a problem, but handling all six of them would've been tough without my sword in hand. Still, most Unusuals were decent enough folk if you showed them a modicum of respect. I had little experience with shark shifters, but I figured they'd react like any group of pack animals and back down in the face of an unknown threat until the advantage was in their favor.

My phone was still plugged into the charger on the passenger seat. I checked the map on the screen and watched for my turn up ahead to get to the rental property. I had little fear that Chip would've skimped on the accommodations. He was a lot of things, but cheap wasn't one of them.

The directions took me to a three-story duplex. I pulled up on the street, parking out front since Chip's SUV occupied the lone parking spot next to the property. It didn't look like the neighboring accommodations were occupied at the moment.

I grabbed my luggage from the Firebird's trunk and walked up to the front door. I tried it, but it was locked, so I knocked. No one answered.

Chip had said if they weren't home when I arrived, he'd leave one of the house keys in the SUV's glove box. I knew the keypad code for the driver's door, so I retrieved the key and let myself in.

The place seemed nice enough as I walked inside. Typical beach furniture of a wooden sofa and two matching chairs were set up in front of the large flatscreen just inside the door. That opened up into a big dining area and then a kitchen at the back. I checked the fridge. Chip had gone shopping and had remembered my Diet Coke cans. There was a chilled twelve-pack waiting for me in the fridge.

I smiled at the consideration. I hadn't asked, but he'd remembered, nonetheless. Who knew, maybe in another life, there would have been hope for something more there.

I carried my bags upstairs. Chip had texted me to take the room with the double bed across from the bathroom. I chuckled as I passed Addy's room. He'd only been here for two days, and it already looked like a cyclone of little boy's clothing had hit it.

I set my suitcase on the bed and called Chip, setting the phone to speaker so I could put away the clothes.

"Hey, Rose. Are you here?"

"I just got inside the house. Where are you?"

"At the beach, of course. That's what we're here for, after all."

I resisted the urge to correct him. The fake vacation was a pretense to get away from home until Sadie could learn to control her wild magic outbursts.

"Okay, maybe I'll join you."

"I brought you a chair out here already," Chip said. "I figured you'd want to come chill after your long drive. Go out the front door and hang a right. Walk until you get to the ocean. We're almost directly straight off the end of the street."

"What are the kids doing?"

"Addy is currently constructing a seawall of sand. He's trying to protect the castle he built earlier from the incoming tide. Sadie met some girls her own age yesterday. She's down at the water's edge with them."

"Good," I said. "I'm unpacking, but I'll put on my suit and come down."

"That would be nice. I've got a cooler here with both beer and Diet Coke, so you have a choice. See you soon."

He hung up, and I returned to my clothes. The room was cramped, even with just the small dresser and a double bed. Still, I didn't plan on doing anything but sleep up here, so it would do. I laid out my suit and grinned. I was a sucker for a good beach trip, and it had been too long since I'd had the chance. There was no way I was going to plain-Jane my suit choices just because of Chip. Besides, it would be fun to catch the look on his face when he saw me.

10

Chip

I leaned back into my beach chair and enjoyed the view of the waves. Making sure I could see both kids, I relaxed with both my charges in view. Rose should be here any minute. I'd rented four wood-and-fabric folding chairs and two umbrellas from the beach vendor the day before. The weekly rate wasn't too bad, and he promised to have them set up for us right where we wanted them when we showed up each day.

The steady breeze flowing in from the water cooled things off nicely under the hot June sun, especially when I was in the umbrella's shade. I had to be careful and manage my time out from under the umbrella. I burned quickly in the sun, and sunscreen never lasted as long as you expected.

That reminded me. I reached into the top of the backpack and rummaged around until I found the lotion.

"Addy, take a break and come up for some sunscreen. You haven't put any on since back at the house."

"But the waves are coming in. My castle—"

"Will still be there if you stop arguing with me and hurry. Rinse off the sand in the water and come here." I held up the bottle and waggled it at him.

He groaned but did as I asked, running over to where I sat.

I squeezed some out onto my hand. "I'll do your back and neck. You can do your front and arms. You'll be done before you know it."

He held out a hand, and once I squeezed white lotion into it, he smeared it on his chest. "What about Sadie? She should get some, too."

"She and her new girlfriends put some on a little while ago when they were lying out in the sun." I added another dollop to my palm and squeezed some out for Addy, too.

As promised, it only took a couple of minutes to slather the boy in the protective coating. I closed the plastic cap on the bottle and dropped it into the backpack.

For some reason, Addy still stood there with his back to the ocean.

"Go on, kiddo. Save your castle from the waves."

"Aunt Rose!" The boy's excited shout relayed his affection for his aunt. He ran up the beach behind me.

I twisted around in my seat. It would have been hard to miss her. Every person who liked the female form had likely noticed her. My eyebrows shot up as I took in her two-piece, pale green bathing suit. A short, flowered sarong was knotted around her waist.

My feet dug into the sand as I pushed off to stand, but I forgot where I was and stood up into the broad umbrella instead.

"Ow," I said, rubbing at the place where my head had knocked against the wooden slats that extended the canopy.

From the broad grin on Rose's face as she walked up, I figured she'd seen the whole thing.

"You okay there, Chip?" Rose asked.

"I guess I didn't expect, well… you." I gestured at her from head to toe. "I'm so used to seeing you in jeans and kick-ass boots that I didn't expect this."

"It's not like you haven't seen all this before."

"Oh," I said. "I remember." I pointed down at her navel ring studded with a diamond and emerald cluster. "That's new."

She laughed. "New to you, at least. I picked that up on an expedition to India about fourteen years ago, a gift from a grateful water sprite."

"Well, I like it. It suits you."

Addy wedged between us, breaking up our conversation. "Aunt Rose, I built a sandcastle, and the waves are coming in. We have to defend it."

"You go get started." Rose tousled his sandy hair. "I'll come help you in a minute. I have to say hi to your sister first."

"Okay." He scampered back to his losing fight against high tide.

Rose turned her gaze to Sadie down at the water's edge. Our niece stood knee-deep in the small wavelets with three other girls, laughing and smiling at boys that walked by.

"How's our girl? Have there been any more incidents in the last few days?"

I shook my head. "It's been quiet. We came out on the beach yesterday. She met one of the three girls then. She's the blonde. Her name's Mills, and she's a local. She brought two of her friends back today to join them. The redhead is Benni, and the awkward brown-haired one with glasses is Adella."

Rose stared at the girls with an intensity that might have been considered rude if anyone had been watching.

"What are you doing? They're not dangerous; they're just little girls like Sadie."

"First off, Chip, Sadie is almost a grown woman in most senses of the word. The sooner you wrap your head around that, the better." Rose turned back to watch the quartet by the water. "Second, all three are Unusuals. Mills is definitely a werewolf from the local pack. She may not have started shifting yet, but there's an aura about her, nonetheless. I'm not entirely sure about the other two. Both have an aura of magic about them. I'll need to chat with them to be sure."

I looked at the three friends with fresh eyes. Opening up my Guardian senses, I let what I saw flow through that part of me. My fingers traced the gold shark's tooth pendant on my chest. I couldn't see the clear auras like Rose could, but she was right. There was something otherworldly about them. I couldn't believe I hadn't seen it before.

"Weird. How did they know to make friends with each other? What are the odds? Sadie has mostly human friends at home."

Rose said, "We Unusuals all have a sense of each other. Sadie's noble Fae nature would have been obvious within a few minutes of interacting with the other girls. Others naturally want to gain favor with the high Fae. It's a custom that goes way back in history when they needed our help to hide from the humans hunting them."

Sadie twisted around as if she'd sensed us talking about her. Her face brightened instantly, and she waved for the other three girls to follow her.

"Aunt Rose," she said. She gave her aunt a hug and stepped back. "These are my new friends. This is Mills, and Adella, and that's Benni." Sadie pointed to each girl as she spoke.

"It's nice to meet you, ladies," Rose said. "I understand you're all from around here?"

"Yes, ma'am," Mills said, speaking before any of the others. "I rarely make friends with the weekly tourists, but Sadie said you're here for the entire summer, so I said what the heck, you know?"

"I do, Mills. Please, just call me Rose. Ma'am just makes me feel older than I am."

"Okay, sure."

Benni said, "My granddad owns the arcade down the boardwalk from here. We were just talking about going over there. Can Sadie come with us and play some games? We won't be gone long."

I looked at Rose, taking my lead from her on this. "What do you think, Rose?"

"I guess it will be okay. Make sure you have your phone with you at all times, okay, Sadie?"

I was surprised that was settled so easily, so I just said, "Have fun, girls."

Mills tugged at Sadie's arm. She and Benni led the way, with our girl right behind.

Before she followed them, Adella's mouth quirked into a half frown, then she did a sort of curtsy without the skirt to go with it. She nodded her head and ran off to join the other girls.

"Well, that was weird," I said.

"The girl's from a family of seers, if I don't miss my guess. She can see flashes of things about people. She may have seen something about

Sadie, but since she's not of age yet, it's probably nothing. I, however, can't hide my nobility as easily without preparation. She knows we're special in some way, at least."

I didn't like the sound of that. "Should we follow them? You know, to be sure?"

"No, my sense of the girl is nonthreatening. The dangerous one in the group is the blonde. She wants to be in charge and have all the power. That's probably why she brought her two friends here today, to show off the new high Fae girl she made friends with. She's the one we'll have to watch."

I looked down the beach until the girls made it to the beginning of the boardwalk and mixed into the crowds enjoying their vacations.

Down by the shore, Addy exclaimed, "Aw, man." The advancing waves had come in far enough to eat away at his central fortress.

I grabbed my phone from the bag and zipped it into the pocket of my swim trunks. It was completely waterproof, and I wanted to take some pictures. "I need to help Addy with his sandcastle. Get yourself settled here with the chairs and umbrellas. This is our home for the coming weeks. We may as well make the most of it."

Rose set her tote down by one of the chairs and untied her sarong. "I'm not above getting my hands dirty. Let's go and try to save the prince's castle for a little longer."

My eyes widened at her volunteering to come right after she got here. I was sure she was dead tired. "We'd be happy to have your help, milady." I bowed and led the way down to the shore's edge.

Dropping to my knees, I started scooping out a deep moat in front of the main castle wall. I had to work fast between the rising waves.

Rose worked opposite me, and we not only made a quick moat but also a secondary wall in front of it before the next wave reached us.

"Good work," I said. "That'll buy us some time." I smiled over at Rose. A smudge of sand streaked her cheek from digging so vigorously.

She smiled back and returned to clearing out the moat after the encroaching wave partially filled it again. We worked alongside Addy for over an hour before a larger wave overwhelmed everything and overtopped the central wall.

It knocked me to the side and sent me floundering for a way to get up as I lay there laughing. Addy and Rose had both seen it coming and had jumped up to back away. They laughed along with me.

Rose reached down to offer a hand up, which I took.

"Well, I'm all sandy and wet now. I guess it's time for a swim. You two want to join me?"

Rose looked around at our chairs and umbrellas. "Sadie's been gone for a while. Can you sense her?"

I reached out and stared up at the boardwalk in the distance down the beach. "Yeah, she's that way. It feels like she's having fun. Her emotions have gotten a lot more complex lately."

"Yeah, that happens," Rose said. "If she's good, then I'd say a swim and a rinse in the water to get all this sand off me is perfect." She sprinted into the water. "Last one in's a rotten egg!"

Addy got the jump on me and plowed into the waves after her, with me close behind. It was shaping up to be a great summer. All we had to do was keep Sadie calm and avoid anything that would release the growing wild magic within her. That should be easy enough.

Rose

After a few hours, Sadie walked back down the beach with her new friends in tow. The sun had tipped back to the west in the late afternoon. They stopped to talk to a teen boy standing on the sand by the lifeguard for a few minutes before returning to their spot on the beach.

I stayed in my chair, out from under the umbrellas to get some sun. "Welcome back, ladies. I wondered if I was going to have to come track you down for dinner."

"No, we knew what time it was. We were having a good time. That's all."

Chip pointed to a cluster of plastic bags with a logo on the side. "The Gay Dolphin? What's that?"

"It's the most awesome souvenir shop. I could spend hours in there. There's so much to see."

Mills said, "It's a fixture here in Myrtle. I figured I had to show it to her."

Benni glanced at her phone and said, "Hey, it's late. I need to get home."

Mills and Adella both nodded.

"Text me if you think you can come back tomorrow," Sadie blurted out.

I winced inside. It sounded a little needy to me, but the other girls didn't seem to notice.

Benni said, "I have to check with my mom. I'm supposed to work a few days this week at the arcade with my Pop Pop."

Sadie brightened. "Maybe Addy and I can come up to play some games while you're there. You can show us the best ones."

"I can do that. You can meet my grandfather." She nodded at me and Rose. "You should all come. I know he'd like to meet you, too. He likes when new folk come to town and stay a while. He says it's what keeps our shore town alive."

I said, "He must be very wise. We'll all come up then."

"I'm good to come to the beach tomorrow," Mills said. "What about you, Adella?"

"I might have a thing to do. I have to talk to my mama." She didn't raise her eyes, even though I tried to catch her gaze. She was hiding something.

I'd have to keep an eye on this one, too. I'd told Chip there was nothing to worry about, and I was pretty sure she'd keep our secret, at least from the other girls. Her family of Seers was another matter. Of course, with them it was all mystery, smoke, and mirrors. They probably had a foretelling predicting Sadie's arrival.

I said, "If there's a chance, Adella, I'd love to meet your mama while we're here. Tell her so, okay? I'd consider it a personal favor." That kind of message would get through to her family, for sure.

"Certainly." Adella bobbed her head in a little bow again, but she didn't do the curtsy, at least.

The three of them waved as they left. Mills and Benni walked side by side, with Adella trailing a step behind them. Hierarchy was important to Unusuals. It told me a lot that even though Mills acted like the alpha in the group, she shared the lead with Benni, whom I'd determined was one of the Mer folk. I wondered if there was more to the mermaid girl than I'd seen initially. We'll go meet her Pop Pop tomorrow.

I leaned forward, standing from the low chair with a groan. "It's late for us, too. We should head back."

Chip smiled. "I'm surprised you lasted this long. You have to be exhausted."

"I've needed a trip like this for a long time. I'd forgotten how it feels to let go like that and just be."

"Well, good then," Chip said. "I'm glad you came out and joined. You deserve a break after all you do for us. Right, kids?"

"You bet," Addy said. "Aunt Rose is the best." He came over and wrapped me in a sandy hug.

"Hey, you're covered in half the beach. Go rinse off in the water again while we gather up our things."

Addy ran back to the water's edge. Sadie helped us gather up our towels and odds and ends.

We each loaded up with our share. Chip pulled the wheeled cooler behind him. Addy yawned big and wide as we walked back up the beach toward the road. He'd played hard all afternoon and was going to sleep well tonight.

Before I could stop myself, I caught a big yawn of my own behind a hand to my mouth as a blue new-model Mustang pulled up on the short beach road. The passenger window wound down, and the driver leaned over to look out as we passed.

"Hey, Firebird. Fancy running into you here." It was the motorcycle gang leader from earlier.

I froze and instantly wished I was wearing more than I had on in that moment. I turned and made myself smile. "Fin, wasn't it?"

"That's right. You staying with these folks?"

"I am. Where's the Harley?" I expected the rest of his gang to cruise around the corner any second.

"I'm here to pick up my brother's two kids. The oldest is a lifeguard for the city, and his younger brother likes to hang out on the beach with him when he doesn't have work to do."

I laughed at his nephew's job before I could catch myself. "One of your kind, a lifeguard? That's kind of counterintuitive."

"Why?" Fin said. His brows lowered, and he flashed his pearlescent teeth. "Because we're all mindless predators bent on random slaughter? It's not our fault we get a bad rap in the movies and on TV.

Besides, a kid's got a right to make a buck, and there are worse things he could be doing. I'm proud of him."

I held up a hand. "Sorry, I shouldn't make assumptions. I figured after our encounter earlier today—"

"That's alright, Firebird. For what it's worth, I wouldn't let that asshole Flick clean up before we left the parking lot. I told him he should think about how close he came to becoming a fish flambé."

I burst out laughing. "Okay, fair enough. Call it even?"

"Deal. This your family?" He waved out the window at Chip and the kids. "With a car like yours, I didn't figure on you being the mom type."

I could've lied and clamped a lid on Fin's flirtatious banter by saying Chip was my partner and these were my kids. But I didn't. What the hell. I enjoyed the attention.

"Sort of. I'm their aunt. This is Chip. We're all staying down here for the whole summer."

"All summer, huh?" Fin's grin broadened. "That's good news."

Before I could agree with him, the lifeguard that had been near us earlier jogged up from the beach with the young teen boy in tow. "Hey, Uncle Fin. Sorry if you had to wait for us."

"No worries, kids. Get in."

The lifeguard opened the passenger door and flipped the seat forward. Before the younger boy got in the back, he waved at Sadie. "Hey, Sadie. See you tomorrow?"

She beamed back at him. "Sure. See you then."

He climbed in, and his brother jumped in the front seat. Fin waved goodbye to us and slipped on his sunglasses, then drove off with his nephews.

Addy crooned. "Sadie's in loooooove."

"No, I'm not. Take that back." Sadie punched her brother in the arm.

Her red-faced reaction told me her brother was onto something. Chip shot me a look. He'd noticed, too.

I needed to nip this in the bud right now. "Sadie Proctor, that boy is probably not the kind you should hang out with. He's a shark shifter."

Chip gawked. "He's a what?"

"You heard me," I said. I moved my gaze back to my niece. "His kind can't be trusted. How one of them got a job as a respectable lifeguard in this town, I do not know. That will be something I check into."

"He's nice enough. Mills and the others know him. They introduced me earlier." Sadie shrugged. "Besides, aren't you both always telling me it's not right to judge people by what kind of background or Unusual clan they come from? How's this different?"

"It just is," I said. "Come on. I'm hungry and tired."

Chip said, "I think we're all tired from a long day. Your aunt is right. Let's go back to the house and get some dinner. Food and a good night's rest will do us all some good."

Sadie marched after me. "I'm not a kid who'll just forget something because you change the subject."

I didn't answer. I was kind of hoping she was. But I had a feeling she would not let this thing with the shark boy go, and I didn't like where that might take us. Sadie charged past me, and Addy scampered after her.

Chip and I brought up the rear, trying to keep up while hauling the cooler.

"He was an interesting character," Chip said. "Are you sure you aren't imprinting somebody else's shark-boy obsession on Sadie?"

"Believe me, Chip, if I wanted to go out with Fin, I could. But that wouldn't set a very good example, would it?"

"I guess not." He stopped for a few long seconds before adding, "I'm glad we're all here together for the summer. I know there's a lot to deal with regarding Sadie, but there's also an opportunity to work on… other things."

I caught his sideways glance at me when he added that last bit. The inference wasn't lost on me, and my initial reaction wasn't all negative. Chip had changed a lot over the last nine years with me and the kids.

The kids raced ahead to the house. Another car had parked in the driveway on the other side of the duplex. The other renters must have returned or maybe had just shown up. We'd have some neighbors after all. Sadie and Addy were talking to the newcomers' kids already.

As we got closer, I spotted a familiar sticker on the SUV's bumper.

My Kid's an Honor Student at Westside Middle

Damn, it couldn't be.

Patty Peyton walked around the back of the car, pulling a small collapsible wagon full of groceries. Sadie stood on the porch of our side, chatting with Astrid, Patty's daughter. Addy and Clayton, Astrid's brother, sat on the steps looking at Addy's pile of seashells.

"Chip, I wondered when I'd see you." Patty's huge, gleaming grin shined out, poorly hiding the obvious intent behind her words. "Oh, hello, Rose."

Chip shifted from foot to foot and kept his eyes down. "You didn't mention you owned the other side of the property, too. I assumed it was rented by someone else."

"No, we own the entire house. We only rent one side and keep the other side for us. After hearing you and the kids were staying here all summer, I asked Astrid and Clayton if they'd like to come down for a month or so. Astrid couldn't wait to get packed. Surprise."

I stared at Chip. Patty owned this house? "Surprise, indeed," I muttered under my breath.

"What was that, Rose?" Patty asked.

"Nothing worth repeating," I said. "I'm sure the kids will enjoy having people they know next door. You're only staying for a month? Don't you have to work these days?"

"Oh, I sweet-talked my boss into letting me work from home for the summer, so I'll play it by ear and see how the summer goes." Her eyes lingered on Chip for a long time.

He didn't break his gaze away from her, either. Something twisted a little inside me. So, that was how it was going to be? Suddenly, Fin didn't seem like such a bad option for me. Chip appeared to have sharks of his own circling. If that was the way he wanted things, fine. I'd already stepped out of their way before.

Without saying anything else, I walked past the two of them and up the steps into our side of the house. I unpacked my beach bag, pulling out the wet towels and things I wanted to hang on the line out back. My hands trembled as I worked.

Chip came in a few minutes later. Sadie and Addy had gone upstairs, and we were alone.

"Rose, I didn't know she was coming, I swear. I would have told you."

"It doesn't matter, Chip. You didn't tell me who you rented the place from in the first place. That tells me all I need to know."

"Only because I know how you feel about her. I never expected her to swoop in and horn in on our summer vacation."

I whirled on him and poked him in the chest. "Well, while you're dealing with Patty's attentions, remember why we're really here. Sadie's going to have another wild magic flare, and it's going to be a lot harder to cover for her with Patty living next door like this." I stalked off toward the stairs. "Figure this out, Chip. I'm getting a shower. You can fill me in later on how you plan to manage this."

12

Chip

Rose barely said two words at a time to me for the next several days. We went through the motions, taking turns watching the kids and otherwise staying out of each other's way. Every time I tried to think of a way to make it up to Rose, Patty magically appeared on the scene with some excuse to insert herself into the situation.

On the third day, we were all preparing to walk down to the board-walk for dinner and some arcade time. Benni had mentioned something about a laser tag tournament nearby, too. Apparently, her grandfather owned several places that catered to the vacationers who streamed through Myrtle beach each summer.

"Come on, kids," I called up the stairs. "I'm hungry."

"Coming," Sadie responded. She bounced down the steps, followed by her younger brother.

"Good, now we're just waiting for Aunt Rose." I checked my watch.

"I'm right here, Chip. No need to hustle me along." Rose trotted down the steps in a cute sundress that was not her usual attire at all. I stared and caught Sadie staring, too. A huge grin spread across our niece's face.

"Aunt Rose has a date."

"Aren't you coming to dinner with us?" I asked.

"Yes, but afterwards, Fin is picking me up near the arcade to take me around and show me some of the more interesting sights around town."

"I thought you'd decided he and his kind were too dangerous."

Sadie frowned. "Yeah, Aunt Rose. You said—"

"I know what I said, and it stands for you and that boy."

"That boy has a name. Conroy's nice, and he likes to talk about the same things I like to talk about."

Rose said, "He's too old for you. He's already in high school, and things move more quickly up there."

"It's not like that. We're just friends."

I grabbed the keys to the house from the counter. "Rose is right. Take things slow, Sadie. It's good that you're just friends, as you say. There's no reason you can't see him at the beach when you're with other kids." I opened the front door and held it while the others filed by. Sadie gave a dismissive sniff as she marched past. Addy was absorbed in a game on his phone, and Rose passed with a familiar wafting floral aroma that always brought a smile to my face.

I locked the door and rushed to catch up before the others got to the corner and turned right toward the boardwalk.

The main drag was busy this time of night. People in sports cars and other convertibles drove by with their music blaring. Interspersed between them were groups piled onto golf carts slowly cruising the boulevard. Everyone was out for the beginning of a fun-filled evening at the beach.

Rose led the way down the sidewalk until we got to an open park next to a large Ferris wheel. It was the kind with enclosed, air-conditioned cars that could hold entire families to go up and see the city from high above the beach and boardwalk.

We walked through the park to where the boardwalk shops began and passed some restaurants until we reached the arcade. Conroy stood outside with Mills, Benni, Adella, and Astrid.

Benni waved when she saw us. "Hey, Sadie, come into the arcade with us. Conroy has a shot at a high score on the Zombie Quest game."

Sadie looked at Rose and me, pleading with her eyes.

I said, "Sure, we can get dinner after we play some games. But we leave when I say it's time to go, okay?"

"Thank you, Uncle Chip." Sadie bounced along over to her friends and went inside. Addy looked my way, and I nodded. He skipped after his sister.

Rose scowled. "I don't like her hanging out with that boy."

"She's not. She's with all her friends. Besides, we'll be right there. Nothing's going to happen."

There were only a few others inside besides the kids. Our group of teens had all clustered around a tall console with a plastic gun affixed to it by a cable. The side read *Zombie Quest*.

Conroy stood behind it and shouldered the gun. He fired at the broad screen, taking down zombies with careful, rapid shots. I had to admit, he appeared to be pretty good at this game.

Addy got some money from me for a token card to play some other game nearby. Rose stood to the side, her eyes never leaving Sadie.

That was when it all blew up into a nightmare come to life.

Astrid moved close to Conroy's side, and when he killed a particularly tough boss, she hugged herself into his muscular arm and reached up to stroke his shoulder.

Behind her, Sadie's sapphire-blue eyes flared and glowed. I knew it was trouble when the hairs on my arms stood on end like they had at the school a few weeks before. A howling rush of wind came out of nowhere and swirled around the group of kids by the game.

"Chip," Rose shouted over the howling rush of wind. "Get her out of here." She was right. I was the closest.

The other Unusual kids all took a step back and looked like they were prepared to scatter.

A mottled green arm clothed in tattered grey rags reached out from the game console and gripped Conroy before he could pull away. Then the entire overly muscular video game zombie leaped through the screen and landed atop the boy.

Astrid screamed and took off, running to the side. Two more of the animated video zombies climbed out of the game and shambled toward the cluster of girls backing away.

Benni tumbled a pair of barstools into the path of the approaching undead monsters. One of them tripped and toppled to the ground. The other clambered over the obstacle and kept coming. Mills and Adella had grabbed Sadie, who was stiff and stationary, by her arms. They tugged her backward with the rest of them.

I pulled my sword hilt from its clip on my belt, extended the blade, and charged in between the advancing monster and the ladies.

Mills had partially shifted into her werewolf form. She held her claws out in front of her and snarled at the zombie.

"Get back!" I shouted. I swung at the zombie's head, but it dodged to the side quicker than I expected. These video game zombies were faster than the real-life kind.

Rose charged in and shoved the broken end of a pool cue through the zombie's ear.

The shard of wood came out on the other side in an explosion of gore that splattered all over Astrid, who cowered off to the side. She had her phone out, recording the whole thing.

We'd have to deal with that later. I didn't want any record that might point a finger at Sadie as the cause of this.

I swung at another zombie that had escaped the game. I only half completed the cut through its neck. It continued its charge at Benni, who backpedaled away from it.

A familiar keening yell sounded, and Addy ran in from the side. Yelling out his battle cry, he launched off the bench of a hungry hippo game and kicked out at the advancing zombie. His extended foot connected with the lolling head with enough force to tear it the rest of the way off.

The headless zombie took three more steps before it tumbled to the side.

Addy bounded to his feet in front of the mermaid girl, his fists at the ready to defend her. It would have been cute if it wasn't so dangerous.

I looked for a safe place for everyone and pointed to the door in the nearby corner. A sign read *Staff Only*. "Girls, Addy, everyone into the office over there. Now."

Sadie, her hands quivering, had returned to herself. She reached out and pulled Addy with her. Astrid jumped up and joined the group as they ran for the office door.

I looked around for Conroy to offer help, but he had gotten free of the one attacking him and was nowhere to be seen. I hoped he was safe and hiding somewhere. More zombies clambered out of the game.

Right before the fleeing children reached the office door, it swung open, and a gray-bearded, very muscular man came out. He wore Bermuda shorts and a pale blue tank top. The stranger wielded a trident, of all things. He moved to the side and let the girls enter the office past him. Then he bellowed a war cry that sounded eerily like a whale song.

He lunged at the nearest zombie racing after the fleeing girls. The tines of the trident pierced the zombie's chest, and power coursed down the metal shaft into the creature. A second later, the shriveled, blackened remains of the beast slid off the weapon to the floor.

Rose and I squared off back-to-back against a trio of circling zombies. These looked to be the last who'd come out of the Zombie Quest game. There weren't any others in sight.

I used my Guardian shield to hold back their attacks, swinging my sword past it to try to puncture their brains when they got close enough.

Rose used the half pool cue to great effect. She had zombie gore up to her armpits. Her weapon dealt death with nearly every attack she landed. A lunging stab with the broken pool cue took out another one as we rotated.

Trident man—whoever he was—strode forward with his weapon leveled at his hip. Once again, power rippled down his arms and into the metal shaft. This time, he didn't wait to skewer a zombie. Midnight-blue arcs of energy blasted out and blew apart the top half of the creature nearest me.

I flinched and swung my shield in place just in time to avoid the worst of the splatter of rotted flesh.

Before we could attend to the final zombie, the gray-bearded man blasted it away from existence, too. He thumped the base of the trident on the concrete floor. Its power resonated through my shoes. I didn't know who this guy was, but he possessed strength beyond any I'd faced before.

Rose let out a long breath. She straightened and faced him. To my surprise, she dropped to one knee and bowed her head. "Your majesty. We thank you for your intervention on our behalf."

Seeing the newcomer in a fresh light, I had flashes of watching *The Little Mermaid* movie with Sadie as a little girl. The glowing trident was the last clue. I went down on one knee, too. "Yes, sir. What she said."

The man, who must have been the king of the Mer people in these parts, walked over to stand in front of us.

"Rise. We mustn't show off for the humans. They'll wonder about things better left unseen." His deep bass voice somehow held the rumble of the waves in it.

Rose and I stood. I said, "I need to check on the kids. One of them might be injured."

The trident lowered, blocking my move to go past him. "First things first." He looked to Rose. "You must be Allura's niece. Your name's something floral, isn't it?"

"Rose, sir," she said. "She contacted you about us coming?"

"Yes, she said you'd reach out when you arrived. I didn't expect you to bring this kind of trouble with you."

"We had an, uh, incident," I said, extending my hand. "I'm Chip, the family Guardian."

He took me in from toe to head, gave a nod, and said, "Well met, Chip the Guardian. Do me a favor and stow that sword. People will have surely called the local authorities by now. We mustn't give them a reason to ask unpleasant questions."

I held up the sword and silently commanded it to go back to wherever it went when it wasn't there. I clipped the remaining hilt cylinder back onto the belt in my shorts.

He snapped the fingers on his free hand, and the gleaming metal trident flared once more and then winked out of existence.

"There, now that's done with, let's get this mess cleaned up. We only have a few minutes to get rid of the worst of the body parts." The Mer King walked over to another door and pulled out a large-wheeled garbage cart. "Put everything in here."

The three of us started in on the cleanup. We got the bin full of bodies and parts shoved back into the janitorial closet just in time. A quartet of Myrtle Beach's finest charged in, their hands on their gun belts, ready to draw.

The Mer King held up a hand. "It's all okay now, officers. As you can see, we had some local vandals come in and try to scare off my patrons. They were covered in fish guts and wore zombie masks, or some such. See, they slopped chum buckets all over my games."

The sergeant looked around, taking in the splattered gore with a doubtful eye. "I don't know if I believe that. There are a lot of upset tourists out there. I'm gonna have to write this up, Ben."

"I understand. Let me call the Chief as soon as I finish cleaning things up." Ben walked to the exit door, talking with the four cops. He left with them to stand outside while Rose and I waited in the trashed arcade.

13

Rose

Chip and I waited while His Majesty talked to the police officers outside. As soon as the police left, the Mer King returned. He locked the doors and walked over to the two of us. "I can cover this up with the local authorities for now. We have an understanding about strange occurrences that happen. The less they know, the better."

"Thank you," Chip said. "Ben, is it?"

I shot Chip a hard look at the familiarity with which he addressed the king of the Mer people. He ignored my glare.

"Yes, King Benedict the Fourth, to be exact. My granddaughter, Benedicta, will be the fifth of our name to rule when I'm gone."

It took me a second. "Ah, yes, Benni. We've met her. She's a remarkable young lady."

"She is. I'd like to have her get to know her future counterpart among the Fae." Ben gestured to the carnage splattered all over his machines. "Judging from the power I felt from inside my office, I assume she's one of the girls in there with my granddaughter?"

"Yes," I said.

"Then let's meet her. We royals have to get to know each other."

I shook my head. "No one else knows her identity but the family,

Chip, and her brother. We need to keep her true identity a secret for a little bit longer."

Ben stared down at me. His eyes flared with a flash of sea-foam white, and a tremendous pressure pushed at my mind. I pushed back with all my Fae might, flaring my own power in my green eyes. I was Fae royalty, and I wouldn't be pushed around like this, especially not to endanger my niece.

Chip stepped between us, his hands pressing us apart. "Now, now, this is not the time or place for another fight. Rose, I believe this is my decision as the Guardian."

"Chip, don't you dare," I warned. This wasn't the place for him to play fast and loose with the rules the way he liked.

"Rose, I've got this."

Ben said, "So, you agree to the meeting, Guardian?"

"Of course. I can be as reasonable as the next person. There need to be a few things worked out first."

"Like what?" He crossed his arms. "I don't enjoy waiting when I demand something, Guardian."

"Please, Ben, call me Chip. It's simple. We send the others home, so it's just family. These things are best kept in small groups, don't you think?"

"That's it? Then we can be introduced?" Ben asked. He closed his eyes and turned his face to the closed office door. "Yes, the wolf girl and the seer can go home. I assume the other Fae noble is the future queen's attendant, and the boy is the prince?"

I said, "No, the other girl is noble, but not part of the court at this time. She must go, too."

"I'll go and tell them to leave," Chip said. "We'll keep Sadie and Addison here with us. You can ask Benni to stay behind, too."

Ben nodded.

I went over to the office door and pulled it open. The kids huddled inside in a group around Sadie, who sat in an office chair at the far end of the room. From her bleary, bloodshot eyes, she'd been crying.

"Kids, it's time to go. Benni, your grandfather asked you to stay here. Go out and see him. Mills and Adella, you two should go home. Can you take Astrid back with you and drop her off with her mom?"

Benni left, but Astrid crossed her arms. "I want to know what happened out there. I felt—well, something. It was wild and terrible, and it happened right before those zombies attacked. Someone did this to us. Is someone going to explain what happened?"

"Talk to your mother about it, Astrid," Chip said. "We'll fill her in on any details we learn when we come back tonight. Right now, it appears to be a random outbreak of wild magic."

Adella shook her head. "Those don't just happen. I've studied them."

I bit back my initial anger. Chip had a new saying he'd been using: *Never argue with toddlers or teenagers.*

I said, "Adella, I suggest you look up your studies some more at home. The owner of this arcade has asked for you to leave. I don't think your elders would want you to anger him, do you?"

The quiet girl's eyes widened. She looked at the floor. "No, Miss Rose. We'll leave."

Mills had shifted back to her teen girl self. Her t-shirt was a little ripped, but she looked okay to go. She jerked her head toward the door, and Astrid and Adella followed her out.

Sadie looked up with tear-filled eyes. "Aunt Rose, I'm sorry. It all happened so fast. I couldn't control it."

I reached out with my thumb and stroked a tear from her cheeks. "It's okay, kiddo. Why don't you find the restroom? Then I want to introduce you to someone important. Addy, go and find the boys' room. You need to wash up, too. You have blood on your face and hands."

He held up his hands to look at them. "Cool."

"No, not cool. Gross. Go wash up." I shook my head and followed the pair of them out. I walked over to where Chip now stood with the Mer King and his heir.

"Benni," Chip said, a broad smile on his face. "You were holding out on us. You didn't tell us you were local royalty."

She shrugged. "It's not something I like to brag about. My Pop Pop likes to make more of it than I do."

Ben spread his arms wide. "That's because all of this will someday be yours, and you have to understand how it all works together to keep the balance. Part of that will be to work with others like yourself. That is why I want you to meet someone."

"Is it Miss Rose? We've already met."

I smiled. "No, it's not me. And I suppose the correct word is reveal. We have something very special to tell you. Can you keep a secret, Benni?"

"Yes, of course."

Sadie returned, along with Addy. They stood on either side of me. I decided it was time and took a deep breath.

I nodded out of respect to Ben and Benni. "Your Majesty and Your Royal Highness, may I present to you both, in an official capacity, Sadie Eldersdottir Proctor, the Queen of the Fae. Or at least she will be in a few more years."

Benni beamed. "Sadie, really? I've never met another royal girl like me before."

Sadie let a hint of a smile pass by her somber visage. "I hope you're not angry I didn't tell you when we first met."

"No, of course not. I don't like to tell people about my connection to the throne, either. They treat me differently when they know. Like with Mills. The only reason she hangs around me is because she knows who I am." Benni shrugged. "She thinks I don't know, but it's pretty obvious sometimes."

"What about Adella?" Sadie asked. "She's around you a lot, too."

"She knows, but she and I have been friends since we were very little, before my parents died."

Sadie's eyes widened. "Your parents died, too? Like mine and Addy's?"

"It was a long time ago," Benni said. "My Pop Pop and Oma have raised me ever since. I don't remember them much."

Sadie reached out and took one of Benni's hands in hers. "Same. It's hard sometimes, but we have Uncle Chip and Aunt Rose to look after us."

Ben cleared his throat. "Ahem, yes. I, too, am pleased to meet you, Queen Sadie."

Addy giggled. "She's not queen yet."

"Indeed," Ben said. He corrected himself. "I shall call you Princess Sadie for the time being, then."

"I guess that's all right, Your Majesty," Sadie said. She mimed a half-curtsy.

Chip added, "Just not in front of anyone else."

"No, I will respect your traditions and keep the secret. But I would like to present her in some official way to my nobility."

I didn't like the sound of that. "If you corresponded with my Aunt Allura, you know the reason we came here was to hide."

"Ah, yes, the wild magic problem. You're hoping the well of wild magic in the Gulf Stream will help mask our young princess's surges. How long do you expect them to continue?"

That was a very good question. I thought back to my youth. With me, it had lasted a month or two, but with Sadie and her increased power, it could be longer. I decided not to hedge and to tell the truth.

"I don't know for sure. Until we know what is triggering the outbreaks, I can't help Sadie tamp down on the feelings behind it."

"Perhaps I can help. My powers come directly from wild magic." Ben looked at Sadie. "What was going on when you felt the power surge through you?"

I didn't like him asking her directly like this, but I couldn't tell the King not to do so on his own turf.

Chip, however, didn't mind bucking traditions. "Sadie, you don't have to answer him right now. This has all been so stressful. We can talk it out after dinner back at the house."

Ben frowned. "How do you expect to sort this out if you don't question the girl? Let her answer me."

Chip squared off and put an arm around Sadie's shoulders. "No, I don't think so. I'm the Guardian. That has very specific responsibilities. I must insist that this be handled our way."

Ben and Chip had a brief staring contest. Ben blinked first, to my amazement.

"Very well, but if there are further outbursts that endanger my subjects either here on land or in the sea, I must insist we press the questioning."

Chip said, "We'll cross those bridges when we get to them. As to this meet and greet with your nobles, is there a way to do it so they meet Sadie without really knowing who she is?"

"You mean like hidden inside another event?" Ben brought his hand up to his chin. "That is an interesting thought. I suppose we could invite all the local Unusual leaders and nobility to a gathering and include visiting dignitaries like yourselves."

"There's my debutante dance later this summer, Pop Pop. What if we made that an open court event where others could come and attend?"

Ben's eyes twinkled. "You will make a very shrewd leader someday, my dearest. A debutante's party, complete with the trappings, and dozens of young nobles to present at once. My nobles can meet Sadie, knowing only she's one among many." He clapped his hands. "Imagine their surprise a few years hence, when they discover they've met you before and I knew who you were all along. That is a choice morsel to savor."

I mulled over the idea Chip had proposed and Ben's solution to it. We had to tread carefully with the Mer King. His power was nearly limitless here, this close to his source of mana. Chip caught my eye as well. He shrugged.

I said, "I think that is an excellent idea."

We were interrupted by banging on the glass doors leading to the boardwalk. Fin stood outside with a very disheveled Conroy standing beside him. The shark shifter leader's shouted words carried in through the glass with ease.

"Let me in, Ben. I demand to know what happened to my nephew in there. He told me a very disturbing story."

Ben's shoulders sagged. "I must handle this carefully. The shark folk and my Mer people have an uneasy truce right now, but it wouldn't take much to tumble it into a full-on war beneath the waves if I'm not careful." He pointed in the opposite direction. "Leave through the street-side entrance at the other end of the building. Benni can show you the way out."

Benni nodded. "Follow me. It's right over here."

Chip said, "Thank you for allowing us our discretion with all this."

"You've had your chance, Guardian," Ben said. "I'll expect an explanation soon."

I tugged at Chip, and he followed me after the three kids.

Benni held the door out onto the street and sidewalk. "See you on the beach tomorrow?" she asked Sadie.

"I think so," Sadie said. "I'm exhausted, and my head hurts. I'll text you in the morning."

Benni smiled, and we filed past her onto the sidewalk, mingling instantly with the throngs of tourists. Just another family at the beach, as far as anyone was concerned.

14

Chip

I left Rose downstairs with Sadie when we got back to the house.

Addy came upstairs with me and plopped himself down on his bed.

"What's going on with Sadie?"

"Aunt Rose and I are trying to figure it out, buddy. It has something to do with her royal power trying to come out before it's the right time."

"I'm worried about her," Addy said. He took his job as his sister's future arms master seriously, even if he was only nine.

I tousled his hair. "Me, too, buddy. I guess it's up to you and me to make sure we do our best to watch out for her until she figures it out."

"I can do that." He stifled a yawn behind his hand.

"You can stay up and play your game for a little bit if you want." I knew he'd do it anyway, and I also knew he'd fall asleep with the game on within the hour.

Addy brightened at the suggestion. He snatched his controller from the nightstand. "I won't stay up too late."

"Good. We have a full day tomorrow. Maybe we can finally build a castle that can withstand the tide."

"Uh-huh." The game already had his full attention.

I pulled the door around but didn't close it tight. I'd come up and check on him later and turn off his light after he drifted off.

Sadie and Rose were already deep into a conversation about the night's events when I came back down the stairs.

"Sadie," Rose said. "Why are you resisting my help? I want you to figure this out so you don't hurt anyone."

Sadie sat cross-legged on the sofa with her arms hugging herself. She looked past Rose at the dimming light of the sunset through the street outside. "It's too late for that."

Rose had taken the comfy chair opposite the sofa, so I pulled one of the dining chairs around and sat down opposite the pair of them.

"What's the difference between a piano and a fish?"

Both women turned their baleful stares on me.

I ignored their glares. "You can tune a piano, but you can't tuna fish."

Sadie rolled her eyes and looked back out the window.

Rose said, "This isn't a laughing matter, Chip. Someone could've died tonight."

"But no one did, right? That's something. Besides, there's never a bad time for a dad joke. Sometimes all we can do is laugh when things are tough."

"We'll have to agree to disagree," Rose said. "This is serious, and we're no closer to finding out what is causing the wild magic outbreaks." She looked at Sadie. "What were you thinking about right before the video game started erupting zombies?"

"I don't want to talk about this." Sadie twisted to the side so she didn't have to look in Rose's direction.

I remembered the moment when the wild magic had erupted to life in the arcade. "It's okay to have powerful feelings for Conroy. He's a good-looking kid. I get it."

Rose leaned forward and rested her elbows on her knees. "Is that it, sweetie? Does it have something to do with how you feel about that shark boy?"

Sadie's head whipped around at us, her eyes flaring blue again. Air whipped around her, and the static electric field of the erupting wild magic started once again.

I couldn't let her destroy the house around us. There had to be a way to contain this. I had a crazy idea.

"Rose, keep talking to her and get her to relax."

Pulling in all the mana energy I could, I reached out with my Guardian barrier. I'd learned to shape it and resize it for various types of defense and even targeted attacks. I'd never tried what I was about to do, though.

Envisioning a cylinder like a soup can, I molded the invisible force and tried to wrap it around our girl on the sofa. Immediately, the wild magic tore at my barrier. Flares of painful fire lanced through my mind, but I held on. I lowered the shield over the spot where Sadie sat on the couch and held it there.

Beads of sweat popped up on my forehead from the exertion. My mana stores depleted faster than ever before. The wild magic was almost too strong, threatening to overwhelm me. I realized two things in that moment: If I didn't hold onto my shield, the backlash would kill me. And the resulting explosion of released energy would likely destroy the first floor of the house and everyone in it.

Rose had moved to kneel beside Sadie. Her palm pressed against the invisible shield, and she leaned in to whisper words to calm Sadie.

I couldn't hear what she said over the rush of pulsing magic in my head. Whatever it was, it appeared to be working. Sadie put her hands to her face, and the swirling bands of blue and black magic thinned some. All I had to do was hold on a little longer.

With all the mana in my personal well nearly used up, I reached out and drew in some from the natural world around me. This was a technique Rose had worked on with me. I wasn't very good at it. Rose said it took growing up in tune with nature like the Fae did to use it properly. Still, I was able to grasp at some of the energy nearby. It pulsed with the current of the ocean's waves and left a taste of salt in my mouth. The infusion of fresh mana buoyed my stores enough to hold on longer.

Slowly, the bands of swirling magic inside my force field thinned into mere wisps of gray and white smoke. I gasped and let go of the field, hoping the wild magic wouldn't rebound. I had nothing left in the tank to stop it if it did.

Rose felt the barrier fall. She reached out and gripped Sadie's hands in her own. She walked forward on her knees and pulled our girl into a tight embrace.

"It's going to be okay. We know what is happening now. We can find ways to control the reaction. All right?"

Sadie nodded once and laid her head on Rose's shoulder.

Rose's eyes shifted to meet mine. She mouthed the words, *You okay?*

I nodded. My forearms rested on my knees, propping up my torso to keep it from collapsing in exhaustion. Every nerve in my body pulsed with the waves crashing on the shore a block away. Somehow the connection to the sea had remained even when I had cut off the mana flow.

Sadie whispered, "I'm a freak, and I'm going to turn evil and kill someone." Her voice cracked at the end. "I should go far away from all of you."

"Hey, now," Rose said. "What kind of talk is that? What would your uncle and I have to do if you weren't around?"

"She's right," I added. "You're the reason we work as a family."

Sadie lifted her head from Rose's shoulder. "But I'm hurting people."

Rose held Sadie at arm's length to look her in the eyes. "That's why we have to work to get control of this magic. It's yours to use and wield as queen someday. Once you get a handle on it, you won't have to be afraid of it anymore."

"But it's not like the magic you've taught me to use already. It's like there are no handles to grab and manipulate."

The pulsing waves in my head and the memory of Addy and I digging moats to direct the ocean water played through my mind. "Maybe there are no handles."

Both Sadie and Rose looked my way.

I shrugged. "What if this wild magic energy is like the ocean? You can't contain it. All you can do is channel and redirect it in a way that is useful."

Rose cocked her head to one side. "Where did this come from?"

"Just now, when I had to reach out and pull in natural energy to supplement my mana to hold in Sadie's magic. I connected to the sea somehow. I can still feel it. It's awful, powerful, scary, and yet it's also full of potential. Not good or bad, just potential."

Sadie said, "So, it's not evil?"

Rose said, "Magical energy is no more evil than the wind or the water. Sure, those things can cause substantial damage and injury, but not through any malice. It's the purpose we put behind magic that makes it take different effects."

I decided to try something. "Sadie, I'm going to ask you about earlier tonight. I want you to use the meditation skills you've learned as part of your martial arts training to keep your thoughts and emotions steady, okay?"

"I'll try." Sadie's eyes didn't convey confidence.

Rose said, "Are you sure this is a good idea, Chip?"

"We'll find out. If not, we wreck Patty's summer playhouse."

"Well," Rose said with an evil grin. "Since you put it that way."

Sadie leaned back on the sofa and rested her hands, palms down, on her knees. She took a deep breath and nodded. "What do you want to know?"

"When I say the name Conroy, what do you feel inside?"

Sadie tensed. She took another deep breath and blew it out slowly. "I feel confused. Like, why does she like him?"

"Why does who like him?" Rose asked.

"Her. She was my friend first. She's supposed to like me."

I said, "You mean Astrid?"

Sadie sucked in a sharp breath and then another. Her chest heaved as she tried to control the emotions inside. Her head jerked in a single nod. She blew out her breath, trying to get control.

I struggled to understand. Astrid had been at the school that day, too, when the boy had been hurt. Astrid was here now, and the magic had surged again.

"Do you need to talk to Astrid?" I asked. "Maybe if you tell her you met Conroy first—"

"That won't do any good. He doesn't matter." Her shoulders quivered as she struggled to control her power. With a whisper, she said, "Astrid matters."

Rose met my eyes, and I saw what I hadn't seen before. It wasn't that Astrid liked a boy. It was that Astrid liked *boys*. I saw the understanding in Rose's eyes, too.

Rose reached out to brush a strand of Sadie's hair back behind her ear. "It's hard to like someone like that when they don't like you back the same way."

I said, "Have you talked to Astrid about this?"

"No," Sadie said. "How could I, especially after tonight? She'll think I'm a freak."

"Why?" I asked. "Because you like girls? Tons of people do, both girls and boys."

"No, because I can't control this power inside of me. Astrid isn't just beautiful, Uncle Chip. She's just about perfect. Astrid can do spells better than me. She's more popular than me and has everything in control."

Rose shook her head. "I promise you, no matter how it looks on the outside, Astrid is just as fearful and confused as you are. It's part of being thirteen. I'll bet she says the same things about you to her mom."

I said, "You know Astrid's mom and I are friends, right?"

"You're not going to share something weird, are you, Uncle Chip?"

I laughed. "Only that I've heard Miss Patty talking about you in an admiring way. She's repeating what she hears from Astrid. Maybe you two should talk about this."

Sadie pulled up her legs and hugged her knees to her chest. "I couldn't tell her I like her that way."

"You don't have to if you don't want," I said. "Try talking about the magic part instead. Right, Rose? That's okay, since they're both Fae."

"I guess so, as long as you don't let slip about your access to so much wild magic, or your future self."

This felt like a good place to end our talk for now. "Good, so we have a plan of action. Sadie, honey, why don't you go and wash up? Once you splash some water on your face, you'll feel better. Then you can read or watch videos before bed."

"Okay." She got up and stopped for a second. "Thank you. Both of you. I don't know what I'd do without you two."

My heart warmed even more. She was such a sweet kid. "We're a family. We'll always be here for you."

Sadie went upstairs. There was even a little bounce in her step.

"That worked out pretty well," I said.

When Rose didn't answer, I noticed she was on her phone.

"Who's that?"

"It's a text from Fin. He still wants to meet up tonight. He's got questions about what we saw. I think I'm going to go for a walk on the beach before heading up to the bar where he's meeting me. I need to think about what to tell him."

I tamped down my disappointment. Rose didn't owe me any explanations, and it wasn't like I was in charge of her love life.

"Have fun and be careful. There are monsters out there."

Rose smiled and grabbed a light jacket from the hook by the door. "Chip, the monsters should be scared of me, not the other way around."

She left, and I settled down for a streaming series I'd wanted to catch up on. After all, there was nothing wrong with staying home alone, right?

15

Rose

I walked up the street until I crossed into the narrow stretch of dunes leading to the beach. The path was marked with slat and wire fencing to keep people from destroying the dunes and the sparse vegetation that helped with erosion during storms.

Once I got to firm sand, I took off my flip-flops and walked down to where the cool water lapped up on the beach. The sand pressed up between my toes, helping me connect to the natural power of the ocean's inherent wild magic.

Chip had mentioned he felt the connection, too, after he used his Guardian powers to help contain Sadie's outbreak inside the house. I didn't think it was possible for a human to build that kind of connection, much less draw upon it to bolster their mana stores. Even after all these years together raising the kids, there was still a lot to learn about how the Guardian magic worked. I wondered how much Chip kept from me.

I wasn't alone on the beach. There were a few people walking together, including a few couples here and there ahead of me. There was only one other dark figure about fifty yards behind me. Their hoodie was up, and it shadowed their face so I couldn't see even with my night vision. It was a powerful figure, though, tall with broad shoulders.

The boardwalk lights up ahead shined like a beacon, marking my destination. I just had to walk a little farther, pass under a pier, and turn right to reach it. I picked up my pace a little. I didn't know why, but something about the hulking figure walking behind me set off warning bells in my mind. I'd learned to trust my instincts.

Running away wasn't in my nature, though, so I jogged along until I reached the pilings supporting the pier and walked into the deep shadows beneath it. Once there, I pulled in my magic and wrapped the shadows around me, obscuring my position behind one of the thick wooden vertical logs.

The shadow figure picked up speed as soon as they lost sight of me. I knew it. They were following me. Time to find out who it was. It could just be a random goon preying on women. If that was the case, I was going to be their worst nightmare. This woman had claws.

The hooded one slowed right before walking beneath the pier and stared into the shadows. Their gaze passed by my position twice before they decided it was safe to proceed. The cool ocean breeze wafted the odor of rotting fish and salt water my way. I thought I knew who this was.

As they passed by my hiding place, I kicked out and down at their nearest knee.

The figure yowled in pain. The leg buckled, and they stumbled forward, trying to stay on their feet.

I darted out and launched into the air, kicking out to the side at the middle of the broad, muscular back.

This knocked my would-be assailant to the sand.

I dove on top of them, rolling them over, straddling them with my knees. My hand cocked back by my ear, ready to drive forward into the exposed throat if needed.

Flick, the shark shifter from the gas station, stared up at me. His eyes widened, and he yelled, "No!"

"Why not? You were following me so you could jump me in the dark, right?"

He shook his head. "I was just following you. I wanted to find out some dirt to expose you to Fin. You're up to something with the Mer King. I was playing pinball in the arcade earlier and hid in a storage closet when everything happened. I overheard part of your conversation with old Ben in the arcade. Fin should know what it is. He and that merman don't get along."

"What did you hear?" I feared he'd heard us talk specifics about Sophie.

"I heard you planning a big party. Something that would likely exclude those considered undesirable by fancy pants like you Fae and the merfolk."

"That's it? You think you deserve an invitation to a debutante ball?"

He squirmed beneath me. "Yeah. I don't know."

I hid my relief that Sadie's secret was safe. I didn't want to have to kill this guy, but I'd do anything to protect my niece. "This is all about payback. You have a grudge to even up with me. Admit it."

Flick shook his head. He stopped as my hand clenched tighter beside my ear, ready to strike. He dropped his chin in a quick nod. "Yeah, I do, but it's better to discredit you than to fight you and maybe lose. I did some checking on you with some dry-land friends I have. You have a nasty reputation of leaving bodies behind you. I don't want any part of that."

Part of me liked to hear that my reputation preceded me. Another side worried about who was sharing stories about me behind my back. Maybe I'd set Warren on tracking them down when we returned home to Westminster.

I stood and took two steps back. "Get up."

Flick got up. He favored his injured leg. I didn't worry too much about it. He was a shifter, and his kind healed quickly. He'd be mostly fine by morning if he gave it a rest.

"I'm on my way to meet Fin now. Come along and tell him everything you know about me."

"No, he'll be angry with me."

I poked a finger at him. "Exactly. That fact, on top of the lack of any actual information to tell him, will keep your mouth shut. Right?"

Flick let out a low, coughing rumble from his throat. I guessed it was the shark version of a growl.

"If you'd rather, we can finish our fight." I let loose with a very toothy grin. "What's one more body washed up on the beach, anyway?"

"Fin's not stupid. He'll find out what you're up to, eventually. Even if he is sweet on you."

I spread my arms wide. "I'm an open book. All he has to do is ask."

When Flick didn't respond, I grinned, took the win, and walked past him as if I didn't have a fear in the world. It took a lot of nerve to go by and keep my back to him like that. I thought I had the measure of the man, though. He'd be wary around me from now on.

I left him standing there in the shadows under the pier, mulling over his options. A minute later, I stepped up onto the well-lit board-walk, strolling along with all the other tourists out for a night on the town. I enjoyed some people watching as I passed through the crowds until I reached the Captain's Catch bar. A lone guitarist played at the back of the narrow tavern. They piped his music out through small speakers onto the boardwalk to entice passersby. It looked like my kind of joint.

Fin waited at the table outside the front doors where you could sit and enjoy the ocean breeze along with your beer.

"Hello," I said. "Fancy meeting you tonight."

"That was the plan all along. Right, Firebird? At least it was, before you had that encounter at Benedict's arcade."

"What did your nephew tell you?"

"He couldn't tell me much. The whole thing scared the shit out of him. Something about zombies coming out of a video game and attacking him and some other kids. The one thing he was clear on was that you and that Chip guy were there and fought off the attack."

"See, you know as much as I do."

Fin's eyes searched mine. "Maybe. I know you had a talk with Benedict and came to some agreement. Care to tell me what a Fae noble from out-of-town wants with the Mer King?"

"No." I didn't explain myself further. My business was my own.

He waited for many long seconds. The approach of our server broke up our staring contest.

"What can I get you?" she asked me.

I nodded at his Corona. "That'll do for me, too."

Fin raised his bottle. "Bring me another while you're at it. This one's about empty."

"Anything to eat? The wings here are pretty good."

I smiled at Fin. "You hungry?"

He grinned back at me and winked. "Among other things."

The comment got a laugh from me that caught me by surprise. I said, "Bring us an order of wings, too. That'll have to do for now."

"Be right back with your beers." The server left to tell the bartender what we needed and to place our food order.

Fin sipped at the dregs of his beer. "You never answered me."

"My family's business is my own. I don't mix business with pleasure."

"Oh, so being with me is a pleasure, is it? That's nice to know."

I chuckled and inhaled. It was strange that I didn't get the stanky fish odor from Fin, just the crisp salt-water of the open sea.

I leaned forward with my elbows on the table. "Answer a question for me."

"Sure, what do you want to know? I'm an open book."

"Why don't you smell all fishy like your fellow shark dudes?"

He laughed. "The answer's not all that interesting, I promise."

I leaned back and waited for the rest of his answer.

"Flossing."

"What? Seriously?"

"Yeah, hygiene isn't a big priority for most of my shark brethren. They prefer to spend most of their time in the water anyway, and don't care how they smell to the landlocked people up here. I take a little more pride in my appearance than most."

"I must say, I approve."

The woman came back with our beers and set a plastic basket of wings in between us. She set down a ramekin of sauce. "That's our homemade blue cheese ranch. It's a favorite. Enjoy."

I picked up a wing and took a bite. It was hot, but not too spicy for me. I turned it around and dipped the unbitten part into the ranch. That would cool it off some.

Fin flashed a toothy grin and grabbed one of his own. "Not too hot for ya, are they?"

"Few things are," I replied. Before I knew what I was doing, I winked at him. My stomach did a flip when he grinned back at me. *Jeez, Rose, why don't you just invite him into the alley over there and get it over with?* I shook my head and went back for another wing.

"What's wrong?"

I finished my wing. "Nothing. You got me to loosen up, and there aren't many who can do that."

"What could you possibly have to worry you so much that you can't let your hair down from that tight little ponytail once in a while?"

"You have no idea." When he just grinned, I continued. "Mostly it's the family business. I search out antiquities to sell to collectors and museums. The responsibilities are a lot sometimes."

It wasn't a complete fabrication, and it would have to suffice. I deserved this. Over the years, Chip had had a string of encounters with Patty and one or two other eligible women around town. I considered myself a lot more discriminating in my romantic choices, especially where it could affect Sadie and her future.

I dipped another wing and pointed at Fin with it. "What about you? You're the pack leader, or whatever you call the head of the shark clan hereabouts."

"A school."

I laughed. "Really?"

Fin shrugged. "I don't choose the language. That's what a group of fish are called. Believe me, I'd prefer pack any day."

"So, what about your school of shark shifters? What kind of beef do you have with the Mer King? It's a big ocean out there. There's got to be room for both of your people."

"It's more about our interactions with the landlocked folk like yourself. The merfolk have a long history of secretly dealing with people on land. When it comes to us, though, people are so scared of us, they swim away before we can ever get to where we're making deals."

"You're saying it's about sharing the business opportunities, that's it?"

Fin raised his beer. "We'd like a little respect. Benedict considers himself in charge of anything that comes from the water around here. He gets annoyed when enterprising groups come up with ways to make a buck that don't include him. Add in that a school of sharks is really just a loose collection of individuals, some of whom I have no control over, and it's a real hassle getting ahead."

He took a long pull from his drink, like he was trying to get an unpleasant taste out of his mouth.

I wondered about my own preconceived notions about shark shifters. Maybe this needed more investigation.

"I think I'd like to learn more. Care to go for a walk?"

Fin dug in his jeans for his wallet. He pulled out a hundred and waved our server over. "This should cover it. Keep the change."

"Thanks." She made the bill disappear into her apron. "You two have a good night."

I said, "We're planning on it." I reached out and took hold of Fin's hand. A pleasant shiver passed down my spine as we touched.

He must have felt something, too. He drew in a sharp breath and looked over at me. "My bike's over there. Want to skip the walk?"

"You're reading my mind." This kind of night had been too long coming for me. Maybe I should be more like Chip and let myself go more often.

16

Chip

I got up before the kids the next morning. While I made pancakes for the family, I called upstairs to see who wanted chocolate chips in theirs.

"Me," Sadie answered.

"Me, too," Addy said. He ran halfway down the stairs.

I stopped him. "Go tap on Aunt Rose's door and see what she wants." I returned to the stove. It was a new one with a cast iron griddle in the middle of the four burners. I melted some butter on the griddle. It sizzled instantly, ready for the batter.

I ladled out four rounds of batter onto the griddle and started sprinkling some semi-sweet chocolate morsels on the still-wet circles. I picked up the spatula and waited to flip them.

Sadie came down and sat at one of the tall stools behind the kitchen island. Addy climbed up on the stool next to hers.

I flipped the pancakes and spun around. "What did your aunt want?"

"She wasn't in the room. The bed was made."

I turned my back and faced the stove so the kids couldn't see my grin. *Good for you, Rose.* "She probably got up early and went for a walk. That's why the bed was made."

Sadie snorted. "Yeah, that's *exactly* why her bed's made."

"That's enough, Sadie. Big kid thoughts should stay in big kid minds."

"Whatever. I just meant—"

"I know exactly what you meant. Drop it."

Addy's still-puzzled expression relaxed me a bit when I turned back to them. Sadie had gone back to looking at her phone.

I finished the first four pancakes, and I put two on each of the kids' plates and slid them over in front of them. "Not too much syrup, Addy."

"Okay." He picked up the plastic bottle, upended it over his short stack, and squeezed out a huge glop on top.

"Hey," Sadie said. She grabbed the bottle from him. "Save some for me."

"There's plenty for both of you," I replied. I ladled out four more pancakes with more chocolate chips sprinkled on top. I'd make the last few batches plain. They could be heated in the toaster another morning.

The kids each went through another plate of pancakes before I sat down next to them to eat mine. "So, another beach day today? We can finally tackle the perfect sandcastle defense."

"Awesome." Addy pumped his fist at his side. "I'm going to change into my suit." He bounced off up the stairs.

"What about you, Sadie?"

She glanced up from scrolling through her phone. "I'm waiting to hear from my friends. After yesterday, who knows if they want to hang out with me."

"Why wouldn't they?" I asked. "They don't have any way to connect what happened to you."

"I guess not." She didn't sound convinced.

"Look, maybe we can try to work through some ways to shift your thoughts when you feel that sort of flare up coming on. If we can redirect your feelings to something positive, maybe you can control what happens."

"I don't think I should fool around with the power without Aunt Rose here."

"I was able to contain it last night. I'll see if Miss Patty can take

Addy down to the beach with her this morning. He and Clayton can play together."

"Then we can stay here and practice some." She finished my thought. "I guess that's okay."

"Good. I'll drop a text to Patty to see when she's heading out. You can do me a favor and clean up the dishes. I'll do the stovetop. It's still hot."

She huffed a little at being given a chore but hopped up and gathered the plates to put in the dishwasher.

I texted Patty.

She replied immediately.

What happened yesterday with Astrid at the arcade? We need to talk.

I frowned and tapped out a reply after a few seconds of thought.

I can meet you out front. We shouldn't discuss this in front of the kids.

I got up. "Sadie, I'm going out on the front porch to talk with Miss Patty. Make sure your brother puts on some sunscreen and has all his things in his tote bag."

"Okay, then we can try what you talked about?"

"Yeah, for sure. As soon as he leaves."

I walked out the front door onto the small porch. It adjoined the porch next door with a low railing between the two. Patty already stood next to it. She sipped at her mug of coffee, though she didn't smile when I walked out.

I tried to shift things to a lighter subject. "Hey, Patty. Can you take Addy with you and the kids to the beach this morning? Sadie's running late getting ready. I'll come down with her in a little bit after she gets herself together."

"That's fine. Clayton is happy Addy's here to play with him. Astrid wants nothing to do with her little brother, so he's lonely." She sipped at her coffee again and said, "About yesterday. What happened? Did you see something that caused the attack?"

"No. I'm just glad Rose and I were there to protect the kids when it happened. We were able to get them into an office while we neutralized the problem."

"What exactly was the problem, Chip? Video game zombies don't just come to life. We both know that's not how that works."

I shrugged and donned my best clueless face. "Beats me. The owner is some sort of merfolk. He thought it was a type of wild magic associated with the Gulf Stream nearby." That was the best version of the story I could come up with quickly.

Patty's eyes narrowed. "That was what he told me when I went back over there to confront him. It's not the only such surge that's happened around here. I felt something very close by last night. I almost came over to check if Rose had felt anything."

"Really? I didn't know anything had happened before or after. I only know what the old arcade guy said."

"Chip, you know who that guy is, don't you?"

"Some sort of noble. I don't pay attention to all that Unusual nobility stuff. You know that."

"You should. He's the Mer King himself."

"Really?" I waved it off. "What's he doing up here on land, then? Doesn't he have a palace under the waves or something?"

Patty gestured around with her mug. "This is where all the money and wealth from the ocean is parceled out to those of us on the land. He doesn't just own the arcade, Chip. The king owns many of the businesses and amusements in the towns up and down this part of the coast. He has partners on land to manage them, but he's the actual power behind them."

"Hmm, learn something new every day. I guess I'm supposed to bow to him when I see him again or something?"

Patty laughed when I smirked at the end. "It wouldn't hurt you to show some respect. How else is Sadie going to be accepted in the same circles as Astrid when she grows up? You have to set an example so she knows how to bow to her betters."

I didn't like where this was going. "What exactly is that supposed to mean, Patty?"

She reached across the railing and placed her hand on my shoulder. "Oh, Chip. You should know that as only a half-Fae, she's looked down on by some others in the Unusual community."

I lowered my eyebrows and opened my mouth to snap something back.

"Oh, not me, of course," Patty said. She pulled her hand back. "You know I adore your kids. I just think you should know the realities, especially with her occasional past flare-ups where she loses control, like at that soccer game a few years back."

"Nothing like that has happened in years, Patty." I needed to nip this direction of thought in the bud right away.

"I know that, but our kind has long memories compared to you shorter-lived humans. Some still talk about that soccer thing in certain circles."

I was simultaneously angry with Patty and glad Rose wasn't there. She'd have leaped the railing and started wailing on Patty for saying anything like this about either of the kids, but especially Sadie.

"I'll try to keep what you've said in mind, Patty." I let the coolness of my tone shut down the conversation. "Should I send Addy over when he's ready?"

"We're leaving when I finish my coffee. I'll have Clayton come over and knock when before we go."

"Good enough, then. Thank you for taking him with you."

"Chip, I know you're angry with me. Don't take it personally. It's just the way things are."

"I'll see you at the beach later, Patty." I went back inside without saying anything else. I wanted to speed up time a few years so I could see the smug look on her face disappear when our little half-breed Fae princess became the next queen and Patty had to bend a knee to her.

"Everything okay?" Sadie asked when I walked in with a giant scowl on my face.

"Yeah, just something I read in the news. That's all. Miss Patty can take Addy to the beach. That'll give us a chance to work on our little problem."

Clayton tapped on the front door fifteen minutes later, and he and Addy skipped off down the street with Patty and Astrid behind them.

I clapped my hands together and said, "Okay, let's start with something easy. Rose has worked with you on meditation. I've watched her teaching you. I want you to settle your mind so there's nothing else but the here and now drifting through."

Sadie sat on the couch and crossed her legs, placing her hands on her knees. She took some deep breaths and closed her eyes.

I drew on my mana stores and prepared to contain any wild magic outbreak with my Guardian shield, like I had the previous night. The distant crashing of the waves was still a throbbing constant in the back of my mind, beckoning for me to draw upon that energy again. I resisted the temptation. Hopefully, I wouldn't need it.

"All right, Sadie, I want you to clear your mind and think about Astrid standing alone with no one else around her. Can you picture that?"

She nodded, her eyes still closed.

"Good. How does it feel? Do you feel any of the wild magic?"

"No, I just feel happy she's there."

This next part was going to be tricky. I didn't want to upset my niece, but I had to give her an image to shake up her perception of happiness and peace.

"Now Conroy is there. He's standing with both of you."

Sadie frowned and scrunched her eyes tight. "She's touching him, Uncle Chip. Her hand is on his arm."

The hairs on my arm stood on end. I thought I saw an aura of power outlining Sadie, like the shimmering heat waves coming off pavement in the summer.

"Breathe deep, Sadie. The power is welling up. Can you feel it?"

She gasped and struggled to steady her breathing. "Y-y-yes."

"Grab ahold of it. Wrap your arms around it in your mind and hold on tight."

"It's hard, Uncle Chip. It's so strong, a-and Astrid is smiling at him."

"No, Astrid is smiling at you, her friend. Conroy has walked away." I struggled to regain control of the imagery I was sending to her. "Try to hold onto the wild magic."

"It's got no handles, no weave to grip like magic is supposed to have." A small cyclone of wind whipped around her on the couch.

I remembered how I had used the shield to contain it. It gave me an idea. "Use your internal mana store to wrap around it. Think like how you'd use a funnel or a tube to contain flowing water."

Sadie squeezed her eyes until they were slits, her brow furrowed above them. "I. Can. Almost. Get. Ahold. Of. It."

The front door slammed open. "What the hell is going on here?" Rose shouted.

The distraction pulled both Sadie and I out of the image I'd created for us, and the swirling winds dissipated into nothing within a few seconds.

I rubbed a hand up my forearm. The hairs had lain down again. The wild magic had diminished. "Sadie and I were practicing for the next time."

"Practicing how, exactly? Were you trying to conjure up the wild magic?"

I shrugged. "It's her power, Rose, not ours. She's got to learn to access it and control it somehow. I thought that was the reason we came down here to the beach?"

That took Rose back a step. "Yes, but you shouldn't have tried that without me here to help. What exactly were you trying to do?"

"I thought a little meditative redirection might help us control it."

Sadie said, "Don't be angry, Aunt Rose. I didn't lose control like the other times. Uncle Chip had an idea about how to contain it. I think it'll work. I almost had it."

Rose opened her mouth, then closed it and paused. "Okay. I really wish you'd waited until I was here. Let's go through this again. Show me what you did and let's see you hold onto it this time, because it sure didn't look in control when I walked in."

Sadie shifted her legs so she knelt on the cushions. "I can do this."

I started the guided imagery again. Rose didn't interrupt. Instead, she sat on the chair next to the couch, ready to act if needed. This time, Sadie did better and wrapped up the wild magic in her innate Fae power almost immediately.

The hair on my arms and neck still stood up, so she wasn't masking the energy, but it wasn't threatening to burst out and cause any unexpected side effects, either. When we finished, Rose asked us to repeat the exercise, which Sadie did several times over the next two hours until it was almost lunchtime.

When we finished finally, our girl's hair dripped with sweat. The last time, she'd gripped the wild magic so fast, there was almost no perception of its release.

"Good work. It's a start," Rose said.

A weary smile creased Sadie's face. She lived for her aunt's rare accolades.

I stood. "I'll make some sandwiches to take out to the beach for us and Addy. He should be ready for lunch soon. Why don't you get into your suit and sunscreen?"

Rose got up. "I need a shower first."

I realized she was wearing the same clothes from the night before. "Okay, you can meet the rest of us down at the beach. Bring what you want to drink. I'll have the rest in the cooler."

Rose jogged up the stairs. Sadie grinned from ear to ear, her tiredness forgotten in the light of her aunt's praise.

I high-fived her as I walked into the kitchen. "You did great, kiddo. Help me get lunch together. You're going to need some food to replenish your mana stores."

Sadie joined me, eating half of the deli meat right out of the package while we made the sandwiches. It was a good morning and a positive start to Sadie coming into her true power.

17

Rose

The afternoon at the beach with Chip and the kids was a welcome return to normalcy after my break from my usual rigid self-discipline the night before. My time with Fin was everything I'd hoped it would be. It had been too long since I'd taken time just for me. All these years since Lili's death, I could count my lapses on just a few fingers.

I'd dreaded coming back home and had taken my time leaving Fin's because I'd hoped Chip and the kids would already be out on the beach when I got back. I hadn't expected Chip to be working Sadie through the paces of learning to control her new power.

Chip had said nothing about my overnight stay away from the family. Maybe he saw the hypocrisy of him saying anything after his frequent episodes over the years. Or maybe he was being kind for a change. He was so hard to read.

I sat out in the sun for most of the afternoon, watching the kids play. Sadie and Astrid spent most of the time lying out on beach towels together and chatting. There was no sign of the other girls they had befriended. I knew they all had various jobs around the seaside town, so I read nothing into it. Sadie needed this time alone with her friend from home.

In the late afternoon, about the time we usually packed up, I scanned the beach in my usual threat assessment. My eyes passed over a tall, muscular man in a purple tank top. He walked toward us down near the surf, his head turned to look over the people up the beach from where we sat.

I thought nothing of it until I remembered seeing him earlier, too. In fact, I was almost positive he'd walked by our position on at least three occasions that afternoon. Maybe it was nothing. He could have been staying at one of the nearby resorts and just enjoyed walking, but my internal senses rang alarm bells.

"Chip, I'm going for a walk down the beach. You don't need help packing up the kids if I'm late getting back, do you?"

"You planning on an all-nighter again?" His lips twisted up in the corners with the start of a grin.

There it was. The old Chip.

"It's a walk, Chip. I should be back for dinner."

I wrapped my sarong around my waist and grabbed my flip-flops in one hand and my phone in the other. Then I walked down the beach after the stranger. I'd deal with Chip later.

It took me a bit to catch up to the guy without outright running after him. I didn't want him to spot me following him. I half expected him to spin around and walk back the way he'd come. If he was watching us, it would have made sense.

Instead, he crossed under the fishing pier down the beach and turned up toward the boardwalk.

I walked up after him, stopping only long enough to brush the loose sand from my feet and don my flip-flops. By the time I got up on the boardwalk, I'd lost sight of him. Then I glimpsed his purple shirt turning down a narrow gap between two buildings.

Careful not to let him see me, I ran over to the passage between a restaurant and a gift shop. I peeked around the corner in time to see him enter a door on the left almost all the way through to the street on the far side.

I darted after him until I was outside the door he'd entered. It was the side entrance to a cafe at the other end of the gift shop. Inside, the purple-shirt guy walked through a doorway with steps up to the second floor. I wondered if he had an apartment or room up there.

With nothing to do but wait for him to come back down, I went inside. I bought a broad floppy straw hat from the stand by the cash register and then sat down in the corner. With the hat on, I could obscure my face enough to watch for the shifty guy to come back down.

"Can I get you something to eat or drink?" the teen server asked me soon after I sat down.

"I'll have an iced latte and the croissant I saw in the window."

"Okay, I'll be right back."

I pulled a credit card out of my phone case to pay the bill when the waiter returned. Then I sat back to pretend to scroll my phone and enjoy my order while I watched the door.

An hour and a half later, the cafe had mostly cleared out except for me. There was still no sign of the guy I had followed in here.

I waved at the server.

"Did you want anything else? We're getting ready to close up for the day."

"No, just a question. What's upstairs? I thought I saw a person I know go in that door over there when I came in."

The kid glanced over at the door and then cleared my plate and empty latte. "The owner has a few rooms she rents to townies who work around here."

"Is there another way down for when the shop is closed?" I asked.

"There are stairs on the other side of the building leading back to the boardwalk." He left with my dishes.

I bit back a curse. I needed to go upstairs and check to see if that guy was still there. He might have left, or he might have taken a nap. I needed to know.

Leaving the ridiculous floppy hat on the chair beside me, I crossed the small cafe and jogged up the steps. They led to a narrow hallway with four doors, two on either side.

I checked them one at a time. First was a bathroom and shower. The second was a door out to a balcony and the outside stairs the server had mentioned. From inside the third, a woman's voice sang along with music loudly and annoyingly off-tune. The fourth door was locked. This had to be the guy's room.

There was no one in sight, so I risked drawing on my power. My eyes flashed green in the darkness, and I muttered, "open." I reached for the door, and green fire wrapped around the doorknob and poked into the deadbolt's keyhole. A second later, a soft click told me I was successful.

I darted inside, ready to silence the occupant if he was still there. The room was empty. There was a single bed with a threadbare mattress and no sheets. A rickety wooden chair sat in front of a small table, and there was a low dresser with three drawers beside the table. I sniffed, and my nose wrinkled. The dead fish smell was unmistakable. This was the abode of a shark shifter.

I scanned the room's contents, searching the magical spectrum for any signs of power or arcane energy. I froze when I saw a familiar round wooden coin on the top of the dresser. The red and black pattern on the half-dollar-sized circle was unmistakable. The runes matched the token I'd discovered in Scotland weeks before during my confrontation with the shadowed figure by the inlet.

That couldn't be a coincidence. It meant the room's occupant worked for the one searching for Sadie. I'd had no luck tracking the origin of the symbols down to any one person or group. It could be a simple sigil of the one I'd fought, or it could be part of an entire cabal working against us.

I needed to know more, and that meant I needed to wait for this guy to come back. I looked down at my beachwear in disgust. It definitely wasn't my first choice for stakeout clothing. It would have to do, though. I didn't want to go home and change and miss a chance at catching our guy. I needed to know what he was up to sooner than later.

I didn't want to sit on the stained and disgusting mattress, and that left the wooden chair. I settled back for a long evening, waiting for this guy to come back. Chip would wonder where I was, and I didn't want him to think I'd drifted off with Fin again. I pulled up my phone and sent him a message.

I found someone related to the person searching for Sadie. Keep the kids at the house tonight. I placed wards there that should keep any unwanted intruders out or at least warn you if anyone enters.

It didn't take him long to reply.

Be careful. I've got the kids. We'll stay in and watch a movie. Check in later when you get the chance.

I gave his reply a thumbs up and checked to see if Warren had emailed any updates on his end. He was supposed to be tracking down the small bits of information I'd found in Scotland to see if anything matched up with any of the evidence from Lili's and Bobby's deaths.

Two hours later, I stood to stretch my legs and stare out the window into the small alley on the other side of the building. The long shadows of the sun setting behind a pair of dumpsters filled the pavement below.

The door swung open behind me, and the guy in the purple tank top entered with a paper bag of groceries in one hand and a twelve pack of beer in the other. He froze as soon as his eyes locked with mine.

"I only want to talk with you, not hurt you." I held up the wooden rune coin. "Let's start with where you got this."

He threw the bag of snacks and the carton of beer at me.

I batted aside the improvised projectiles and shouted after him as he ran down the hallway away from his room.

The guy bolted out the door and down the wooden stairs leading to the alley below.

I gauged the distance from the landing to the ground and decided jumping down in flip-flops, dressed only in a sarong-covered bikini, was not smart.

"You're making this harder than it needs to be." I jumped to the next landing and took the final stairs down two at a time. Leaping from the middle of the last flight, I tackled the fleeing shark shifter to the asphalt pavement.

I ignored the skinned knee I got for my trouble and rolled him over.

That put me face-to-face with his snapping shark jaws and multiple rows of teeth.

The good thing about aquatic shifters was, though they had a shifter's enhanced strength, they didn't have many extra advantages if they changed while on land.

I dodged the snapping teeth and brought my knee up between the still-human legs at the bottom half.

A gurgling yelp of pain escaped the shark's mouth, and the shifter tried to wriggle out from under me. His upper limbs were useless fins at this point, and I easily avoided his powerful bite.

Using my forearm, I pushed up on his lower jaw to clamp his mouth closed and punched my other fist into the gill slits beside his head. I punched again and again.

Then, with a powerful lurch, he finally bucked me off and rolled me into the rough wooden siding of the building next door. He shifted back to human form and raced down the alley toward the beach. That told me where he planned to escape.

I couldn't let him reach the water. He'd be far more dangerous—or get away entirely—if he made it to the shoreline.

My long strides kept me close, but not quite close enough. It was so dark now that most people around us didn't realize what was happening as we ran past them.

He dove into the surf just before I caught up with him, and his powerful strokes carried him out past the first breaking waves.

I stopped when I was knee deep in the water. I knew better than to chase him any farther.

He stopped swimming about twenty feet away from me.

"My master knows the power he seeks is here in this town. It's only a matter of time until we discover where you're hiding it."

This guy hadn't been told exactly what his master was seeking. I could use this to my advantage.

"Your master knows better than to come in person. Next time, I won't stop to ask you questions. I'll just kill you."

A small crowd had gathered on the beach behind me. Apparently, my chase down off the boardwalk had drawn more attention than I thought. I needed to get out of here. Someone had probably called the police already.

The guy flipped me the bird with one human arm and dove out farther into the incoming waves. He didn't surface again that I could see, and I was sure he was fully in his shark form now.

I backed out of the water, knowing even the shallows weren't safe at this point.

"He went under and didn't come back up," a female voice behind me said into her phone. "Some lady chased him into the water, and I think he's drowning."

I turned around and ran back up toward the boardwalk. A few people called after me to stop, but no one pursued me. I needed to get away from here, but first I needed to stop back at the guy's room. My phone was still up there.

After I fetched my phone, many questions ran through my mind. I only knew one person who might have some answers. I wasn't sure Fin would give them to me, but I had to find out.

18

Chip

With Rose gone on her hunt, I was left to figure out dinner with the kids. Astrid invited Sadie over to spend the night next door, and I agreed with only a little trepidation. Sadie needed to work through her complex feelings around her friend. Since they were getting along, I hoped she'd be able to do it without another flare of power.

Patty, the four kids, and I arrived back at the duplex, and I set out the beach toys on the porch so we didn't track too much sand inside.

"Chip," Patty said, "the girls are fine fending for themselves this evening. I thought maybe you and I and the boys could have dinner. You mentioned Rose was out for the evening on some errand?"

"Uh, yeah, she probably won't be back anytime soon. What did you have in mind? I don't have a lot in the way of groceries right now."

Patty scrolled through her phone. "There's a rib and barbecue place nearby that delivers. I think the boys will enjoy that. What about you?"

My stomach growled at the mention of barbecue. I'd spent the day at the beach with just a peanut butter sandwich to tide me over.

"Sounds good to me. Why don't you take care of it? I'll have a half rack of ribs and a dozen hot wings if they have them."

"Carolina sauce okay with you?"

I loved the mustard-based barbecue sauce from around this area. "Oh, for sure. Addy likes it, too."

"Oh, good. I prefer it when I'm down here, but Clayton just likes ketchup." She held up her phone. "I'll call in an order and get the girls settled on my side. Then I'll come back. Is it all right if I send Clayton over once he's changed from his beach clothes?"

"Yes, I'll get him and Addy squared away with their video games. That'll keep the pair of them busy for a while."

Patty waved and headed inside with her two kids. Sadie ran upstairs on our side of the duplex to change while Addy and I got our beach stuff put away.

"Addy, go get changed and clean up. Clayton will be over in a minute."

"Okay, Uncle Chip." Addy ran upstairs after his sister.

I changed into a pair of Bermuda shorts and a Hawaiian shirt to match my beach theme for the evening. I don't know why I bothered. It wasn't like I planned on anything happening with Patty. A random hook up would make our summer next door to each other awkward as hell. Still, it didn't hurt to dress nicely, even for a delivery dinner in.

While I was changing, Sadie called in through the closed door, "I'm going to Astrid's."

"Okay, have fun. Don't stay up too late."

I came out from my room a few minutes later and went into the kitchen to chill some glasses in the freezer. That would go nicely with beer when they delivered the barbecue.

A knock at the door stopped me in the middle of clearing off the dining table. "Come in, Clayton. It's open."

"It's not Clayton," Fin said from the open doorway.

"Oh, hi." I stared for a second, unsure how to proceed. "Uh, Rose isn't here right now. She had some late errands to run."

"Oh? I saw her car parked outside and figured she was in for the evening."

I shrugged, trying to come up with an excuse. "Yeah, I don't know when she'll be back. She walked up the beach a while ago and texted to say she'd be out for the evening and to not wait up for her."

Fin checked his phone and shook his head. "She hasn't answered me in a while. Okay, I'll head up to the boardwalk and see if I can track her down."

Clayton walked in the open door behind the shark shifter. "Hi, Mr. Chip. Is Addy upstairs?"

"Yes, Clayton. You can go up. He's got his video games hooked up to the TV in his room."

"Awesome." He ran upstairs and left an awkward silence between me and Fin.

"I guess I'll go." Fin turned to leave and bumped into Patty coming in behind him.

"Oh, hello." Her hand traced down Fin's muscular arm for a second before she pulled it back. "Aren't you that friend of Rose's?"

"Yes," Fin replied. "I was just headed out to catch up with her. Bye, Chip."

I smiled, watching Patty's eyes follow the rough and tumble shark shifter out to his car.

She caught me watching her and laughed. "Some gals have all the luck. He looks like an interesting type. Still, Rose deserves some fun, even with his kind. I think she takes life way too seriously, don't you, Chip?"

"Rose has her priorities straight," I said. "She doesn't need your pity." I don't know why I jumped in to defend her. Rose could take care of herself, but I knew how Patty still looked down on *weird Rose* from high school, even after all these years.

"Rose has her quirks, and she doesn't play the political game that goes on between Fae nobles. As a human, though, you wouldn't understand all that." She scrolled through her phone and showed me an email she'd received. "That is an invitation from the Atlantic Mer King himself. He's invited all local and visiting Fae nobles and other Unusual dignitaries to a ball to celebrate the coming of age of his granddaughter."

"I heard about it. What's so important about that?" I didn't want to let on that Sadie was the real reason for the event, so I pretended to be uninterested.

"Chip, this is a huge deal. And Rose would be on top of it if she was paying attention to what's really important. I tried to tell you before. Sadie is going to have a hard enough time fitting into Fae society because she's half human. This is a rare opportunity to raise her social capital. Does she even have a dress with her to wear to an event like this?"

"Uh, I don't know." Rose and I hadn't talked about it. I was pretty sure Sadie hadn't packed anything even semi-dressy when we left home in such a hurry.

"Exactly," Patty said. "That's what I mean. Rose should do anything she can to find Sadie the perfect outfit for this party. It might be her only chance to make that kind of impression. All the girls their age will be presented to His Majesty, with the Mer Princess herself coming in last of all."

My eyes darted to the front door. I wished Rose were there to counter what Patty said. She'd know enough to derail Patty's line of questioning.

"Don't worry, Chip. I have to do some more shopping with Astrid. If you give me some money, I'm sure I can find something appropriate in a second-hand shop in town."

I'd heard enough. "That'll do, Patty. Now that I think about it, Sadie is already attending and has the perfect outfit picked out, thanks to her Aunt Rose. I'm sure she'll make a wonderful impression on the Mer King when the time comes to present her. You'll see."

I didn't know why I threw in that last part. It wasn't like we planned on announcing Sadie's true identity as the next Fae Queen. She wasn't even close to eighteen yet, and I couldn't trust Patty or anyone else outside the family with that information.

"Well, why didn't you say so? Is it upstairs? I'd love to see it." Patty walked toward the steps to the second floor.

"No, it's getting altered. You know thirteen-year-old girls are hard to fit for things like this. Rose is supposed to pick it up in a few days."

Patty pouted. "That's a shame. I was looking forward to seeing what Rose came up with for the party. Her tastes in such things are, uh, interesting."

"What's Astrid wearing?"

"I've got a beautiful, professionally designed sundress. It's a one-of-a-kind just this side of semi-formal, yet it still gives the impression of a summer vacation soirée. You have to be careful not to wear something that would upstage the guest of honor, yet still be stunning in your own right."

I bit back a comment about Sadie's being better. I didn't do catty very well. "I'm sure she'll look radiant. All the girls will." Seeking to get off the subject of Sadie, I asked, "When will the food get here?"

"It should be here in fifteen minutes. I hear the boys upstairs, and that gives me enough time to bring up another sensitive subject with you."

I didn't like the sound of that. I wondered if she planned on making a move on me and positioned myself with the dinner table between us. "I don't think we should…" My voice trailed off.

"No, silly, this is something serious. It's about *magic*." She whispered the last bit. "Look, you and I have never talked much about your kids' true Fae nature. I've always assumed that Rose would have handled that with you."

"What are you talking about?"

"I've felt strange surges of power when Sadie has been nearby. There was that incident at the middle school. And I felt something again the other evening when you all were next door. It was close, so close that it was unmistakable where it came from."

I didn't like where this was going. "Patty, I'm not sure what you're trying to say. Everything is fine with the kids and their Fae natures."

"Is it? Really? I tasted the wild magic for sure this time. Girls Sadie's age go through a time where they can't control things. I've never felt such power in someone, especially someone who's half human. Astrid has had some flare-ups, but we've worked on learning to control her powers. Is anyone doing that with Sadie?"

"It wasn't Sadie, Patty." I didn't know what else to say. I had to protect my niece. "It was me."

"You?" Patty's jaw dropped.

"You know I've always dabbled in the human side of magic. I've never hidden that from you when we've been together." She thought I was a hobbyist mage of limited ability.

"Chip, playing with the odd barrier spell or dancing fairy lights is one thing, but trying to grab onto wild magic is dangerous. Surely Rose has told you this before."

"I haven't told her. It's something I've been working through on my own. I met some people back home who showed me what to do, and I've been practicing."

Patty stood up straight with her hands on her hips. "Well, stop going in that direction right now. What I felt the other night from over here was more powerful than anything I've experienced before. There's no way you'd be able to control something like that for very long. You're lucky it didn't kill you."

"It was nothing. I tried to tap into the currents coming off the Gulf Stream out in the ocean. It was silly of me, I know. Honestly, though, the power was more than a little intoxicating."

Patty frowned. Then she walked around the table to stand by my side. She put a hand on my shoulder. "Chip, that's the point. Humans were never supposed to harness that kind of power. Centuries ago, the Fae and humans fought wars over control of the wild magic."

"I guess you think I should stop, just like that, and never try again? You know me better than that, Patty. Besides, Rose can help me if I need it."

"Rose doesn't know you the way I do, Chip." Her hand moved from my shoulder and rubbed down my chest. "I know how impulsive you can be. Maybe if you let me help you, it would be safer. We could go down to the beach later and try a simple summoning spell."

I reached up to push her hand away, but the doorbell rang. I looked through the front window and saw a scraggly shirtless teen holding a couple of paper bags on the porch.

"Uh, let's hold that idea for now. The food's here." I dug in my pocket for my wallet. "Did you pay already?"

Patty stepped back and let her hand drop to her side. Her lip pushed out in the barest hint of a pout. "I used my card when I ordered, but you can tip him. I'll go up and call the boys to dinner."

I let out a sigh of relief and went to retrieve the barbecue from the delivery guy. I had an entire dinner to figure out how to get out of the mess I had created for myself. I wasn't sure what I was going to do when Patty wanted me to call up real wild magic on my own. Then she'd know I was lying the whole time.

I decided to eat slowly while I came up with a diversion. It was my only choice.

Rose

I waited at the bar for Fin to show up. His text message was a welcome distraction from my thoughts about the shifter I'd chased. He'd texted me several times earlier while I waited for the other shark to return to his room. I'd held off answering him until after the chase down the beach. Now he was probably making me wait my turn. I'd have considered it a fair trade if I wasn't deadly serious about talking to him about his fellow sharks.

I twirled the floating ice in my drink with one finger. The single malt Scotch on the rocks helped to calm my twitchy nerves after the chase into the water. Maybe I should have gone after the guy. I had a spell that would allow me to swim underwater like a native.

"You're crazy, Rose," I said aloud to myself. I sipped my drink and shook my head. Thinking like that could get me killed. There were only two reasons I'd dive into shark-infested waters, and those reasons were safely in their beds by this time.

"Talking to yourself isn't something most guys look for in a gal," Fin said.

I hid my surprise that he'd entered from the street entrance rather than off the boardwalk. "Good thing you're not most guys."

"True." He smiled and gave me an appraising look from head to toe.

"What are you looking at?"

He snorted a chuckle. "I'm trying to decide where you land on the crazy/hot Mendoza diagonal."

"Be very careful with what you say next, Fin." I swirled my drink and sipped it.

Fin answered right away. "Oh, I already decided. I'm here, aren't I?"

"Yes, you are. I guess if I'm meeting a shark shifter in a beach bar, I deserved that consideration."

Fin slid onto the barstool next to mine. He waved at the bartender. "I'll have what she's having."

The cute blonde behind the bar nodded and tapped in the entry on a tablet slung over her shoulder with a carrying strap. "Be right with you after I finish this order."

Fin got his credit card out and held onto it while he waited. "You're a hard girl to get ahold of for someone who doesn't know anyone else in town."

"Hard to get is still a thing, isn't it?"

"It is. Care to tell me why you chased a member of my school into the waves earlier this evening? That was why I took a little longer to get here. I had to talk the Myrtle PD chief out of tracking you down."

"So, you admit he's one of your people?" I twisted so I faced him directly. This was important. I liked Fin, but I needed to see his face clearly to determine if he was involved somehow with the strange power tracking Sadie.

"He's not one of my favorites, but all the shark shifters in the area are technically in my school. Why, what's he done now?"

I couldn't come right out and tell him everything, but I'd need to give him enough to either link himself to the conspiracy or come to my side.

"He's working for someone I encountered on a recent business trip. That someone is a threat to people I care about. Your guy is connected to him."

"How can you be sure?"

I fished the wooden talisman coin from between two credit cards in my phone case. "Does this look familiar to you?"

Fin took the token and turned the carved wooden disk over in his hand to inspect the runic designs on both sides. "These aren't oceanic runes. They resemble old markings I've seen somewhere else, though."

That caught my attention. "Where?"

"They look a little like Atlantean pantheon runes. Not exactly, but close."

Atlantis was one of the ancient high Fae cities. The gods destroyed it after its leaders dabbled in dark magics. It had sunk beneath the waves thousands of years before. There were only a very few among the Fae who could trace their lineage back to the survivors. After the island's destruction, it was my family who ascended to royal status for centuries afterward. We had ruled until our enemies forced us into hiding nearly five hundred years ago.

Fin interrupted my racing thoughts. "I mention Atlantis and you don't answer me, even with a mocking laugh. Most people don't even believe it ever existed. What's going through that pretty little mind? Do I even want to know?"

I downed the rest of the fiery amber Scotch. "I think some elements of your school are linked to a remnant of that island's royal clan somehow." I considered how it all made sense now.

"Didn't they all die off? I thought they were nothing but trouble. The legends all say that was why the gods destroyed the island."

I nodded. "Their wickedness was part of it. They dabbled in dark arts and had a dangerous connection to a darker wild magic. That, thankfully, has long since died off."

The bartender set Fin's drink in front of him. She brought me a fresh one, too. Fin handed her his card after pointing to both drinks. She took it and tapped it on her tablet for payment. Fin scribbled his signature on the device, and she went to deal with the other patrons.

"So, you believe some of my people are involved with one of these Atlantean descendants?"

"Yes." I picked up the wooden token from where Fin had left it. "This is the only clue I have to their identity. I thought I'd given them the slip by coming here for the summer. Now I know they've tracked us down."

Fin sipped at his drink and studied me over the edge of his glass. "You're here for Ben's protection. His control of the Gulf Stream's wild magic would make him a powerful ally. The question is, why would he help you and expose himself to this Fae squabble?"

I didn't answer him, lost in thought while I worked at my Scotch. I had to tread carefully with Fin. His sharp mind had already drawn too many correct conclusions.

As if to confirm my fears, he continued. "I don't believe for one minute it's you they're after. You're not the type to run from an attack. This has something to do with your family."

"Careful, Fin. You're close to something here that very few people are aware of."

Fin set his drink down on the bar. "What, are you the next Fae Queen in hiding? That old legend isn't true. They'd have found the royal line by now and exposed it to everyone."

I stared at him and thought about whether I should lure him somewhere I could kill him or give up the greatest secret of my life. I weighed both options.

Fin's eyes went wide, then narrowed. He leaned close. "My gods, Rose, that's it, isn't it?" He paused, thinking. "But I already know it's not you they're after. You're not exactly queen material." He snapped his fingers. "The girl."

I leaned forward and worked hard to keep fear for Sadie's safety from my voice. "Fin, you've stumbled on something here that very few people know. I've killed too many who've discovered that secret. I won't let anything happen to her, not even if it's you."

Fin leaned back, his palms out at his side. "You've got nothing to fear from me. I respect the old ways as much as any of my people do. I'll even protect your niece myself if needed. But you're right to fear the renegades in my school. I don't rule them the way Ben rules the Mer folk. I advise and bully, but in the end, every shark's a loner."

He stopped, and a lopsided grin crossed his face. "Ben knows, doesn't he? He'd have to. And that zombie attack in the arcade, that wasn't a random wild magic outbreak. It was your niece."

I twisted my head to see if anyone had overheard him. "Fin, you have to be quiet. I don't want to hurt you."

"I told you. I'm no danger to her. In fact, I'll help in any way I can."

"How do I know I can trust you with this?"

"Because you have to. I'm the only way you're going to find out what my renegades are up to. They don't know I'm doing more than bedding you."

I didn't like the way he put that, but I nodded. "Go on."

"I can try to learn what they're up to, maybe even track down this ancient Fae lord who's after your niece."

"Why go to all this trouble for some summer fling you just met?"

"Do I need a reason to do the right thing? This isn't just about knowing you, Rose. I have a feeling this is important to Ben, too."

I understood as soon as he said it. "And you want to have the Mer King in a position to owe you one?"

Fin shrugged. "It couldn't hurt."

"Fine." I decided I wouldn't kill him for now. I also wouldn't trust him completely. "But there's someone else who has to know you're in the inner circle."

"Let me guess, Chip?" Fin smirked. "I thought you two weren't an item?"

"He's the children's legal guardian, and there's more to Chip than meets the eye. He doesn't appear to be much more than a typical human, but he's come around over the past few years. Come on. Let's go back to the house and see what Chip thinks about everything you've told me."

I downed the rest of my drink in one big gulp. The fire burned on the way down, but I needed it. Trusting Fin felt like the right thing to do, but guys had betrayed me before.

"Which way to your car?" I asked. "I walked here."

"I'm parked on the street out this way." He led me out the entrance he had come through and over to his car. I climbed into the passenger seat while he held open the door. I appreciated the gesture and nodded when I was ready for him to close it. Time to go and see what Chip's Guardian senses thought of letting a shark lord in on our family secret.

20

Chip

I put off Patty's advances after dinner by pointing out the boys could come downstairs at any moment. We couldn't just go back to my bedroom and hope they didn't notice.

Patty pushed out her lower lip a little, but I held my ground. "Sorry, Patty. It's not you, it's me. There's a lot going on with all of us staying in one house like this. I don't think it's a good idea to mix up the vibes for the rest of our vacation."

"If you say so." She walked over to the couch and picked up her purse, her shoulders sagging. "One of these days, I will not be available any longer. I'm in my prime, you know. I'll find someone else if it isn't going to be you."

"And I'll be happy for you. We've had our good times in the past, and I want us to be friends in the future."

Patty's shoulders drooped even more. "Friend zoned at last. Just tell me one thing, Chip. Where did I go wrong?"

"You didn't." Her instant frown told me to keep going. "I'm not feeding you a line, Patty. This just isn't a good time. Maybe there'll be a better time in the future, but you deserve more than a wait-and-see from me."

Patty held my gaze as if searching for some inkling of a lie behind my eyes. She shrugged after a few seconds and called up the stairs. "Clayton, come on. We're leaving. You can play with Addison again at the beach tomorrow."

A minute of awkward silence later, Clayton came down the stairs with Addy a few steps behind. "Mom, do I have to leave? Astrid's having a sleepover. Why can't I stay here?"

I saw a way to make peace with Patty. "He can stay until tomorrow. I mean, you've got the girls over there. I can keep the boys here. We'll meet up again in the morning and switch everyone back. We can even do breakfast with everyone." Having Patty here for breakfast in the morning would annoy Rose, but she'd get over it. She might not even come home tonight if Fin caught up with her.

"Yes!" Addy pumped his fist at his side. "We can stay up all night playing, Clay."

Patty rubbed her chin. "I guess that'll work. Clayton, listen to Mr. Chip, okay?"

"Sure, Mom. Can we go back up and play some more?"

"That's up to Mr. Chip."

I nodded. "You can, but it'll be lights out and bedtime soon."

Clayton and Addy bounced back up the steps while Patty walked over to the front door. "I'll check on the girls before I go to bed. I'm in the room opposite yours on our side if you change your mind. The key's under the mat out front."

"I'll keep that in mind, but I think it's best if I stay here with the boys. Bye, Patty."

After she left, I cleaned up the rest of the dishes from dinner. It wasn't too hard. Most of the dinner leftovers got wrapped up and put in the fridge. It would make a good meal to reheat for a few people. I was washing out the sink when Rose returned. I heard her voice as she entered and looked back to see who she was talking to.

Fin waved as he came in behind Rose and closed the door.

"Oh, hey, Fin," I said. "I see you found our girl."

"Chip," Rose said. "Where are the kids? Are they asleep? We need to talk about something important."

"Sadie's having a sleepover with Astrid next door. Clayton is upstairs with Addy. They should be getting ready for bed soon. They're playing video games."

"Let them keep playing, then. They won't hear us over their headphones. You, Fin, and I have something to talk about."

That intrigued me. I moved over to the cushioned chair and waited for Rose and Fin to sit down on the couch.

Rose never got the chance to say whatever it was she was going to say next. Patty burst through the front door, panting as if she'd sprinted over from her house.

"The girls. They're gone. I've searched the whole place and they're not there."

"What?" Rose asked. "Chip said you were watching them."

"I was over here having dinner with Chip and the boys," Patty said. "The girls were there by themselves for a few hours before I went back. I cleaned the kitchen before I went up to check on them. I thought they were just asleep early because they were so quiet."

In a panic, I reached out with my Guardian senses, searching for that special connection to Sadie. The fingers of my right hand pressed hard against the shark's tooth pendant beneath my t-shirt. Sadie definitely wasn't next door. I reached outward for her location until I spun around a hundred eighty degrees, facing to the Southeast.

"There, she's that way and not close." I pointed in Sadie's direction. There wasn't much in that direction but a line of high-rise condos and then the beach. That worried me.

Rose ran for the front door. "Come on, Chip. We need to find her. I have a bad feeling about this."

"I'll come, too." Fin followed Rose out the door.

"What about me?" Patty asked.

"Stay here," I said. "Watch the boys and be around in case the girls return before we find them."

"They're probably just out meeting up with some boys. It's harmless," Patty said. Her fingers interlaced and twisted with a worry that belied her statement.

"We'll see," I said. "Stay here. I'll call you."

Rose called in from the porch. "Come on, Chip. I need you to find her. I can't do this alone."

I slipped on my sneakers and met them on the porch. I wasn't sure why Rose was letting Fin come along, but I'd learned to trust her judgment. There must be a reason he was there.

My mind tracked around like a radar beacon, homing in on Sadie. As she had grown up, the connection to her had changed a little. It had been blurred ever since her distant cousin took her back in the fourth grade. Something about the magic that had been used to mask her position from me had lingered to this day. Still, I had a general sense of direction and distance. I wished I could pinpoint her location like when she was much younger.

I pointed over toward the boardwalk and started down the street in that direction.

Rose said, "We'll take Fin's car. He can drive and drop us when we get close."

I pivoted in place. Rose held open the passenger door, and I got in the back of the shark shifter's sports car. Rose climbed into the front passenger seat after I was inside.

I pointed up between the seats. "She's up that way. Maybe she's on the boardwalk, but she seems farther away than that."

"I'll take your word for it," Fin said. He gunned the engine and peeled out down the street until we'd turned onto the main drag. Luckily, it was late enough that much of the usual nighttime traffic had passed for the evening.

We paralleled the boardwalk while I continued to point. Suddenly I felt the tug change direction and shouted, "Turn left, here!"

Fin spun the wheel and entered a parking lot with a long fishing pier at the far end. Sadie's location was dead ahead down the pier.

"She's down there and still not that close. She must be all the way at the end."

Rose jumped out and pulled the front seat forward so I could exit, too.

Fin joined us. "I have a fishing pass for the pier. You usually have to pay, but I can get us out there. Follow me."

We joined Fin and let him take the lead. He pulled something out of his wallet and showed it to the attendant. "Hey, Kyle, I'm showing some friends from out of town the sights. Can I take them down to the end of the pier for a few minutes?"

The rotund guy on the stool at the pier's entrance nodded. "Sure. Don't be too long. If you decide you want to go fishing, they'll have to pay the guest fee."

"Gotcha," Fin said. "They just want to see what's down there. We'll be right back."

Rose and I nodded. I reached out, trying to gather whatever information I could from my connection to Sadie. I didn't get a sense she was in fear or danger. She seemed amused and amazed, if anything.

"She's out there and doesn't appear to be injured," I said. "I don't know why she'd come here, though. She's never been fishing in her life."

"We'll find out," Rose said. She pushed past Fin to jog up the ramp and through the pier's arched wooden entrance. I followed right behind Fin.

We caught up to Rose as she hurried to the end. There were a few scattered folks out night-fishing, but there was not a sign of Astrid and Sadie anywhere.

"Where is she, Chip? You said you could sense her out here."

I reached the rail at the end of the pier and closed my eyes to concentrate. When I locked in, I focused on her direction and pointed. She was moving away from me. I opened my eyes and stared down my arm out to sea. My heart sank.

"Is she on a boat?" Rose asked, searching the darkness for some sign of a vessel.

"No," Fin said. "I was afraid of this when we came here. She's with some of my kind. Sadie is Fae, right? She has to have some magic to sustain her underwater?"

"How is that possible?" I asked. Panic set in. "Are you saying she's underwater? She can't be there; she couldn't breathe."

Rose shook her head. "There's a spell that her Fae protection charm could access. I mentioned it to her once, so she might know it. It allows for movement and breathing underwater. She wouldn't be able to keep up with a native like one of Fin's shark shifters, but she could survive and swim well enough."

Fin climbed up onto the railing overlooking the ocean swells. "Rose, I will find her and bring her back to you. This I swear."

I gulped and decided what I had to do. I kicked off my shoes and climbed up onto the railing beside Fin. "I guess it's time to find out if my Guardian charm has the same spell."

Fin frowned. "I can't protect you down there if I'm finding and protecting your niece."

"You protect her and bring her back. But first, you need me to show you the way to where she is."

"You don't have to come," Fin said. He pointed out at the dark water. "I think I know where they're going. There's an old German U-Boat wreck out there. It's right before the drop-off into really deep water. That's where I'd take a girl to impress her. A lot of our young ones like to hang out there."

"You'll still need me to pinpoint where she is. I'm going along." I didn't feel as confident inside. I was a decent swimmer, but this was a whole new thing.

"I'm coming, too," Rose said. She jumped up next to us and dropped her unwrapped sarong and bag behind her on the wooden planks beside the railing. "Don't worry, I'll keep up."

Fin didn't wait for us to say anything else. He dove off the high pier into the water below in perfect form. If I hesitated, I'd lose my nerve. With a deep breath, I jumped out and tried to keep myself straight up and down as my feet pierced the cool water below. Rose jumped right behind me.

I struggled to get my bearings in the darkness beneath the sea. I had to trust my charm. My inner voice wished I could see better in the dark waters. My charm flared with a chill against my chest, and the dark vision spell activated, allowing my eyes to pierce the ocean's gloom a little better.

Two seconds later, I let out an underwater, bubbly scream as I came eye to eye with a twelve-foot great white shark.

A familiar voice in my mind reached out to calm me. *It's me. It's Fin. This is my shark form. Is your magic charm working?*

I wrestled my panic under control and realized I was still underwater. It was then I felt the burning need for oxygen in my chest. I fought against the urge to paddle to the surface. My inner voice repeated over and over, *I need to breathe, I need to breathe.* I repeated the thought and fought down the urge to kick for the surface. Suddenly, the water's drag on my arms and legs lessened.

"Hey," I said aloud, as a strange bubble of air formed around my face and head. "I can breathe again."

"Your charm is working for you," Rose said, her head inside a similar bubble. She used both feet to dolphin-kick past me. "Come on. Fin is waiting for us."

The shark stared at me. *Point out her direction and hold onto my pectoral fins on either side. I can pull you both with me.*

I gripped the massive shark fin, bringing me close to the muscular body. Rose moved around to the far side to do the same. I pointed with my free hand in the direction where I sensed Sadie.

My arm nearly jerked from its socket as the powerful tail beat back and forth behind us, propelling us through the dark waters of the Atlantic, out toward the distant Gulf Stream and this mysterious submarine wreck. I didn't know what to expect when I got there and had no idea how I'd be able to defend myself underwater if it came to a fight. All I cared about was getting to our Sadie.

Then I was going to ground her for life.

21

Rose

The thrill of the water rushing by me as I held onto Fin's impressive shark self might have been a turn on if it hadn't been for the danger Sadie was in. That and the fact that Chip was along for the ride. I didn't know what had possessed Sadie to run off in the middle of the night like this, much less disappear underwater to investigate a submarine wreck. I knew that her growing up would bring on some rebellious changes, but I hadn't expected things to progress so quickly.

Fin slowed some. *I sense some of my kind ahead. There are some from my school, but there are also others there I don't recognize.*

"Don't you have some measure of control in your own territory?" I asked.

I do, but there are limits. Most big sharks are solitary hunters. That lends itself to a certain level of personal autonomy.

Chip's voice sounded like he was calling from the bottom of a deep well. "Are we expecting a fight? There has to be a way to negotiate our way out of this. I'm still not sensing any fear or danger from Sadie."

"We'll stay close to Fin and follow his lead," I said. "This is his territory."

Fin continued his powerful tail strokes, towing the pair of us forward. In a short while, I picked up on a jagged shape rising out of the ocean floor up ahead. That was the sunken sub.

It lay tilted a quarter of the way to one side. A jagged hole had torn open the bow midway back to the conning tower that jutted up from the long, tubular hull.

I searched the numerous shark shapes gathered around the opening, looking for Sadie, or even Astrid. If we found one of them, we would probably find both girls. I couldn't see Sadie leaving Astrid, since she was likely the reason Sadie came down here.

A pair of hammerhead sharks swam up in front of Fin, blocking his way.

What are you doing, bringing them here? the larger shark asked.

Fin answered, *I'm here helping them search for their younglings. I think one of our school brought them here. Am I right?*

The smaller hammerhead said, *You should go back. We'll search for any young Fae girls.*

I didn't say they were females or Fae. You do have them. Where are they? Fin's head turned from left to right to give himself the broadest view of the whole submarine.

A mermaid with a long tail and close-cropped red hair swam by. "Benni," I called.

The young mermaid pivoted when she spotted us and swam over. From her creased brow and frown, I could see she was worried about something.

Chip noticed, too. "What's wrong, Benni?"

She also spoke directly into our minds with no bubble of air to carry sounds. *I came here with Sadie and Astrid. They wanted to see the wreck after Conroy described it to them. He met us near the pier and brought us here. But I went to talk to some friends, and when I came back to where I left them, I couldn't find either Astrid or Sadie. Now there are sharks blocking me from looking for them by the wreck.*

"Chip, can you locate Sadie?" I asked.

Chip swam forward a few strokes past Fin and the two hammerheads as he turned from side to side, searching with his Guardian senses. He pointed at the jagged hole in the submarine's hull. "She's there. I think she's inside the wreck."

Chip and I both swam forward toward the jagged opening. We stopped when a quartet of sharks swam in front of us to block our way. There were the same two hammerheads we saw earlier, a great white, and a tiger shark.

"Get out of our way," I shouted. The force of my exclamation caused bubbles to escape from the zone of air around my head.

The larger hammerhead said, *I said we'd search for the lost younglings. You don't belong here. Go back to the surface now if you want to live.*

I reached to my side for a blade that wasn't there. I was still in my bikini and ill-prepared for a fight, especially here in their element.

Fin slid into position above Chip and me. *They are here under my protection. I don't think you want to cross me, Gil. I've shown you who is the best before, and I'll do so again.*

The hammerhead's broad nose shifted from side to side. *It is you who should beware, Fin. You are alone here. Your school isn't behind you right now. We hold this territory, and it is we who control who enters and who leaves.*

Chip's hand came up. He held the round hilt of his collapsed sword. I wasn't sure how effective it would be, even with our magic spell for protection and relative freedom of movement underwater.

Fin was the first to move. With a powerful flick of his tail, he surged forward, his mouth opening wide.

He never made it to his target.

Just before he reached the hammerhead, a rumbling wave of power blasted outward from the center of the sub. From the chill it sent down my spine, I knew it was another surge of wild magic from Sadie.

A split second later, Chip and I dropped ten feet through a giant bubble of air to the sandy ocean floor beneath us. The air pocket had formed around the sunken ship. All around us, shark shifters had all dropped to flop on the sandy ocean floor until they shifted back into their human forms and stood.

One of them, the smaller of the two hammerheads who'd blocked us, turned into the guy I'd chased into the surf earlier that night. He pointed at the submarine and called to the other hammerhead shifter. "I told you. One of those girls is the chosen one our master spoke of. The reward for finding her is ours as soon as we identify which one it is."

"Chip," I called. "We have to get to Sadie and Astrid." I ran for the open side of the submarine and gripped a rusted metal pipe as thick as my arm. With a twist and all my power, I wrenched it free from the sunken wreck and turned to fend off any who came close with my three-foot length of rusty steel.

Chip ran past me, his sword's blade deployed. He climbed up over the jagged, rusted metal and disappeared inside, calling Sadie's name. I knew he'd get to Sadie and protect her. I just had to give him time to find her.

Gil and the other three shark shifters stood where they had fallen in the sand. Despite their nakedness, they still radiated power here in their ocean. Even with the unnatural bubble of air, they held all the cards.

"This wave of wild magic won't last forever, woman," Gil said. "The waters will return, and then we will have you."

I thumped the rusty pipe in my palm. "Not if I take you out first."

"You and what army? Your partner disappeared inside the wreck."

Fin ran over to stand at my side. "I'll stop you if she doesn't. Back off, Gil. If you leave now, I'll let you go free to find another place to make your home in the oceans."

"Maybe your school needs a new leader." Gil and the other guy took a step in our direction.

Behind them, I spotted Benni pushing herself up to stand on her human legs. "Benni, get your grandfather. Tell him Sadie's in trouble. He'll know what to do."

She waved and ran for the edge of the bubble to return to the water. She took three steps and dove into the wall of the bubble, disappearing into the dark waters behind it.

"Go after the Mer princess," Gil called to the other two standing with them. "Stop her, but don't hurt her. We don't need that kind of trouble from the Mer King. Cutter and I will take care of these two."

The two shifters ran for the spot where Benni had disappeared and dove in after her. I hoped she swam fast and could find her grandfather quickly. We could use the Mer King's help right now.

I hefted the pipe and prepared for the charge of the two shifters. A few other shifters moved in our direction, but most of those who'd been swimming around the wrecked sub either stayed where they were to watch or had bolted for the relative safety of the waters outside the unnatural bubble.

Fin squared off against Gil, which left me to take on the one called Cutter. He had all the inherent power of his kind, even in human form. He would be a formidable opponent. My rusty steel pipe wasn't my enchanted silver alloy blade, and I would need some luck and skill to get through this fight. I had no choice, though. Sadie depended on me, and I had to defend her.

Cutter charged at me and raised his arm to block the pipe I swung at his head.

My attack was a feint, though. I snapped a kick straight out in front of me and caught him in the chest, propelling him away so he fell backward in the sand.

I didn't let that attack stand alone. I charged after him, swinging the pipe to catch him on the shoulder and back as he rolled over and tried to regain his feet.

Again and again, I swung the pipe at the struggling shifter.

My luck ran out when his hand slapped out and caught my ankle hard enough to sweep my legs out from under me.

I hit the ground hard, landing on some coral, which ripped open a gash on my upper arm.

Cutter's eyes flared red at the smell of my blood in the air. His mouth widened unnaturally to reveal row upon row of triangular teeth. He dove at me headfirst, his jaws snapping open and closed.

I jammed the end of the pipe inside the soft skin of his palate and twisted the rough metal end into the fleshy interior.

A bellow of pain followed, along with the odor of rotting fish. He stood and backed away, spitting gobs of blood on the surrounding sand.

"You'll pay for that, Fae witch."

"Come and try to collect, shark boy. I'm just getting started."

He shouted a raging torrent of curses at me and charged again, leading with his snapping shark teeth.

I wound the pipe back and swung it like a bat, caving in his lower jaw completely. The force spun me around, and I reversed my grip to complete a backswing that smashed back into the other side of Cutter's head.

He tried to swivel his head out of the way of the incoming blow, but the bloody wreck of his lower jaw slowed him just enough.

The pipe smacked against the side of his head with a pleasant crunch, caving in part of his skull and cheekbone.

Cutter's eyes went wide for an instant, and then he slumped down, his gaze still staring off past me with lids that would never close again.

Fin had knocked out Gil. He had broad gashes on his forearms but appeared to be mostly okay.

"What now?" I asked.

He nodded at an advancing trio of shark shifters coming to avenge their fallen friends. "You climb up inside while I hold them off."

"There's three of them. They'll chew you to bits."

Fin grinned, showing his own rows of shark teeth. "Not before I rip off a few pieces of them for good measure."

I shook my head. "Nope, we hold them off together and wait for Ben to come. His granddaughter will bring him."

"If she didn't get waylaid by the ones who chased after her," Fin warned.

We both turned to face the advancing shifters coming at us. Behind them, the bubble had shrunk some, and the wall of water was closer than before. I hoped Sadie's magic held out long enough for us to defeat our foes. I didn't like my chances in the water against these sharks in their home environment.

22

Chip

"Sadie, where are you?" My voice echoed down through the dank submarine.

I struggled to push through the cramped wreck. The U-Boat's contents had collapsed into the passageway in some places, creating dangerous and jagged obstacles in my path as I searched. It would have been easier to navigate while swimming, but on foot was a slog.

I pressed on. The shouts of the conflict at the entrance faded behind me as I traveled farther inside.

Sadie's voice echoed from up ahead. "Uncle Chip, we're over here."

"I'm coming, keep calling out." I followed the sound of her voice.

"We're in the part where they steered the ship, I think," she yelled.

She was definitely close. I found a very rusty ladder leading up and called through the hole.

"Sadie, are you up there?"

My heart filled with relief when her tear-streaked face appeared in the opening above me. "Uncle Chip, you found us. Conroy told us to come down here so he could show us this wreck, but then he wouldn't let us leave."

Astrid's face popped in next to Sadie's. "Yeah, he was saying some really weird things, too. Something about wild magic and a missing link."

"Where is he now?" I half expected the teen shifter to slide in between the girls.

"Sadie whacked him on the head with a piece of metal after some weird surge of magic filled the wreck with air. He flopped down to the floor, and she hit him as soon as he shifted back to human form."

Sadie shrugged. "I got lucky and caught him by surprise, and he dropped to the deck. That made it easy to hit him. He's knocked out over behind us."

"Okay," I said. "Let's get you ladies out of here. Aunt Rose is outside with a friend."

The rungs of the ladder between us had rusted almost all the way through. They'd never hold anyone's weight, even someone Sadie's size.

"You'll have to slide over the edge until I can reach your feet. I'll catch you. I promise."

Sadie nodded. Astrid said, "Why aren't you yelling at us? If my mom was here, she'd have let us know how pissed off she was right away."

I pictured Patty sitting at home waiting for Rose and me to return. "You wait, Astrid. I'm sure she'll make you aware of her feelings about running off tonight. We'll deal with the consequences once we have you both safely back on dry land."

Sadie turned around until she was on her stomach and slid over the edge of the hatchway feet first. I stretched up to grab her ankles.

"I have you, Sadie. Use your arms to lower yourself down. I'll catch you."

She did as I told her, and soon I gripped her waist and lowered her to the deck beside me.

"Okay, Astrid, you're next."

"What about Conroy?" the other girl asked.

"He'll be fine. When he wakes up, he can swim back on his own."

"But he's in human form. If the water comes back, won't he drown?"

I hadn't thought of that. I didn't want the boy's death on my hands, even if all this was his fault. I'd let Fin deal with him.

"Drag him over to the edge and push him down so I can reach him."

"Eww, I have to touch him?" Astrid said. "He's naked, Mr. Chip."

"Just pull at his ankles until he's over the edge. I'll take care of the rest."

Astrid disappeared for a few seconds. She returned, pulling a pair of legs over the hatch opening. When she had pulled the feet to the far side, she let go and the unconscious boy slid down through the opening. I scrambled to catch him.

I mostly supported his weight, so he didn't fall to the floor too hard. He groaned, and his hand came up to his head. There was a big welt on the side of his face next to his left eye. I helped Astrid down last of all and then examined the unconscious boy.

The boy's eyes fluttered open and widened. "Hey, what are you doing here?" He crabbed backward against the bulkhead. "Where's all the water?"

"It's gone, for now at least." I drew my blade and extended it to only a short eighteen-inch length. "Are we going to have a problem?"

Conroy shook his head. "No, mister. I just brought the girls down here to show them the wreck, that's all."

"You're lying," Sadie said. "You tricked us and then wouldn't let us leave."

The boy never took his eyes off the end of my short sword. "I just did as I was told."

"Who told you to bring them here?"

"It was my friend's father. He said someone important would reward all of us if I brought both Fae girls here."

Astrid humphed and crossed her arms. She whirled her head away from the kid.

Sadie hauled her leg back and kicked Conroy square between his legs. "That's for tricking us, asshole."

Conroy doubled over, clutching his exposed privates.

I didn't even consider correcting Sadie's language. The kid was an asshole, and probably worse than that, if Rose's fears proved true.

I loomed over the collapsed shifter. "We woke you up. You're on your own. We're leaving. If you try to follow us, I'll gut you and leave you here for the crabs to feed on. Got me?"

Conroy looked up from his curled position and nodded.

"Come on, ladies, we need to get back to the surface. This air pocket is unnatural. I'd like to be out of here before it collapses completely. Let's go find your Aunt Rose."

I led the way back through the debris-filled passageway until we reached the opening to the submarine. Rose was waving a rusty pipe back and forth, menacing a pair of sharks swimming past inside the wall of water, which was only a few feet in front of her. The bubble had shrunk a lot.

"Rose, I have the girls. Let's get out of here."

"Easier said than done." She pointed with her pipe at the two waiting sharks.

I moved to stand beside her with my sword ready. "Where's Fin?"

"He chased after one of the others, who swam off to get help."

"Then I guess we'll have to take out these two and get away before anyone comes back." I leaned forward to stab through the water at the nearest shark, extending my blade's magical length to its full meter. I frowned as the metal appeared to bend as soon as it pierced the wall of water.

"It's just like a spoon in a glass, Chip. The water refracts the light, so nothing is where you think it is."

The shark outside flicked its tail at my sword's tip. The blow nearly jarred the hilt from my grasp. That thing was strong. I didn't relish the moment when the bubble shrank even more and left us in the water with them.

Astrid asked, "Why are they making all this fuss about us? It doesn't make any sense. It's not like we have money to ransom or anything like that."

I cast a glance at Rose, and her eyes met mine. This was not a line of questioning we wanted anyone to entertain.

"I think he was just being a silly boy and causing trouble," I said.

"That's not what he said back there," Astrid said. "He said someone asked him to bring us here. Why?"

Rose said, "We can ask him later. Right now, we have to get you two back where it's safe."

The water had pressed inside the opening and filled the deck around us up to our knees. We were running out of time.

I prepared to sacrifice myself so Rose could make a run for it. I had the only actual weapon in the group. Right before I opened my mouth to tell Rose my plan, the sharks outside spun around and darted away from the opening.

"Where'd they go?" I asked.

"Something spooked them," Rose said. "I don't know what, though. There isn't much that can scare off a grown shark in the water like that."

A pair of shapes zoomed in at us from the darkness outside the ship. At first, I thought it was more of the shark shifters. It wasn't until the shapes got closer that I realized they were dolphins.

The pair sped past the opening in the direction the sharks had gone. Another group of figures appeared behind them, led by a large merman with a golden crown. It took me a second to realize it was Ben in his full underwater royal form. Benni floated behind him, with a dozen other merfolk clustered behind. All were armed with silver tridents.

The Mer King swam up to the opening as the water continued to press us backward. His powerful voice rang inside our heads. *Come out, and we will take you out of here. I know not where this air pocket came from, though I can hazard a guess.*

Rose said, "Thank you for coming so quickly, Your Majesty."

It was high time I put those shark vermin in their place. I had hoped Fin could control his own folk, but I guess that was too much to wish for.

"He protected us, Your Majesty, and helped us find the girls."

Is the princess safe? Ben asked.

"Both girls are as well as can be expected," Rose said quickly.

Very well. Swim through the barrier, Ben said. *Let's get you back to the surface. I sense a coming darkness nearby. I think it is best that we are not here when it arrives.*

I didn't like the sound of that. "After you, Rose. Then I'll send the girls."

She dropped the pipe, and it splashed in the water around our ankles. Then, with perfect form, she dove through the water to the ocean outside.

"Okay, Astrid, you're next."

The blonde girl jumped awkwardly through the edge of the bubble, which shrank even more until it was barely ten feet across.

"I'm tired, Uncle Chip. I can't hold onto it any longer."

I noticed how pale Sadie was. Somehow, she'd sustained the bubble with her tenuous control over the wild magic this whole time.

"On the count of three, let go of the power. Just remember to switch to water breathing."

"What about you, Uncle Chip?"

I tapped the shark's tooth talisman on its chain around my neck. "I'll be fine. This got me down here in one piece. It'll get me back."

Sadie nodded and let her tense shoulders sag. The rest of the bubble splashed in on us, and I took a second to reorient myself to the underwater magic.

Sadie floated limp next to me.

"Sadie!" I called.

The girl is well, Ben said.

A thin layer of air encircled her body.

My people will see her safely to the surface. You and the other two hold onto the dolphins.

Two mermen came forward and lifted Sadie between them, while three dolphins appeared and hovered near me, Rose, and Astrid. We all gripped the base of their dorsal fins.

The powerful tails beat downward and towed us up to the surface. As we neared the top, I saw the shadowy outlines of boat hulls on the water above us. One was large, and two other smaller boats with outboard motors circled it.

I surfaced with my dolphin companion and recognized the red blazon of the U.S. Coast Guard on the larger vessel. The two smaller boats were manned by Coast Guard personnel, too.

Ben had surfaced nearby and talked with the officer leaning over the side of the bigger boat. Hands reached out nearby and pulled Sadie up into one of the smaller boats before retrieving Astrid, Rose, and, finally, me. Then the boat approached the Coast Guard cutter so we could transfer aboard.

Once we were all on the small cutter, the trio of boats headed back toward the shore.

Sadie awakened, though she was still very pale. A medic checked her over and said she was just hypothermic and dehydrated. They wrapped us all in blankets and left us alone in a small cabin with the officer in command of the boat.

"You all were very lucky King Ben was able to warn us you were out here. What possessed you to go snorkeling at night like that?"

Rose's expression darkened at the officer's tone. I leaped in to interrupt her instinctive response.

"You're very right, Lieutenant. We misjudged how much daylight we had left. If it hadn't been for the merfolk and your intervention, things could have been very bad."

That seemed to satisfy him for the time being. "I'll need to document this and get all your names for my report."

"What about the merfolk?" I asked. "Will you mention them, too?"

"There's a classified menu for reporting on Unusual folk like yourselves. Just be thankful he asked us to let you go with a warning. We owe him too many favors to disregard when he asks for one from us. But I don't want to catch you out here again, understood?"

I nodded. I glared in Rose's direction. As soon as she nodded, I added, "Thank you, Lieutenant. That's very considerate of you."

He looked out at the darkened horizon in the moonlight. "There's some bad weather blowing in. Funny, it wasn't in any of the reports from earlier. Just another strange thing on a very weird night patrol."

The Coast Guard officer left, and the four of us had a moment alone at last.

Rose put her fists on her hips. "You girls should know better than to run off with strange boys, especially shifter types. Even the ones on land are nothing but trouble most of the time."

"Yes, Miss Rose," Astrid said. "We know that now. What I still don't understand is why Conroy did it. He said things that didn't make any sense. So did the Mer King."

"We'll talk about that with your mother," I said. "You two don't need to worry about it. This is a matter for the grown-ups."

Astrid frowned but didn't say anything else. Sadie had snuggled up against Rose's side, and I leaned my head back against the bulkhead to clear the worries from my mind until we got back to shore. There'd be plenty to do when we were home in the duplex to deal with what I feared was coming.

23

Rose

The Coast Guard landed me, Chip, and the two girls at their station in Georgetown, just south of Myrtle Beach. We had to sign off on the written report regarding our official statements. The lieutenant used a tablet to collect the signatures from me and Chip as we stepped off the gangway.

"I have your contact information, so we'll be in touch if we need any further updates from you. You're free to go."

I looked around and raised my hands at my sides. "Where exactly are we supposed to go? It's after two in the morning, and we're miles from our place at the beach."

Chip dug in his pocket and let out a burst of laughter. "Hey, what do you know? That waterproof phone case I got worked." He held up his phone to show the screen still had life.

I rolled my eyes. Leave it to Chip to have the expensive and usually useless gadget to save the day. I'd left my phone in the bag up on the pier with my sarong.

"I'll call us a ride share." He tapped on his phone a few times while I waited with the girls. "It'll be here in twenty minutes."

The Coast Guard crew had returned to their duties on the boat and inside their small station building nearby. I decided this was a good time to deal with our two ladies. I wanted to make sure we had the right story in Astrid's mind before we got back to Patty. She'd have far too many questions, and some of them might implicate Sadie if we weren't careful.

"Girls, come over here."

Sadie and Astrid approached, still wrapped in their government-issue mylar rescue blankets.

"What happened that made you decide to sneak out like that?"

Sadie shrugged, but Astrid blurted out an answer.

"Conroy texted us he knew of a really cool place he wanted to show us."

I bit back my initial response and settled on, "So you two went along to where he takes all the summer girls he meets?"

"It's not like that, Aunt Rose," Sadie said. She glanced at Astrid and closed her mouth before saying anything else.

I knew she'd only gone because Astrid was going, but that didn't forgive the error of the decision. It only explained it.

"I know exactly what it's like, Sadie. Look, girls, Conroy and his friends are looking for something in particular, something powerful. They think they'll find it from the two of you. They're wrong, but that's not stopping them from using you to get what they want. Do you understand?"

Astrid cocked her head to one side. "When we got to the wrecked submarine, he said something about choosing between us. I thought it was a boy thing but given everything else that happened when he wouldn't let us leave, I wonder."

That line of thought was the one thing I wanted to divert if I could. I came up with a lie I hoped she'd believe. "Astrid, there's an old legend down here that some magical Fae power can be found if the right one of us is brought along to discover it. It's not true, of course, but some locals believe in it, nonetheless. Fin told me all about it. It's nonsense, but some people will chase after any old legend."

Chip added, "We're not even from down this way, so it doesn't apply to us, anyway. We're not of the local Fae nobility."

"That's true," Astrid said. "But what happened with that blast of magic that made the water go away from the submarine? At first, I thought it was coming from Sadie, but she couldn't have that kind of power."

"No," I said. "Of course not. I think it might have been something the Mer King did right before he arrived. He can tap into the wild magic directly from the Gulf Stream. He probably wanted to save you girls, along with Chip and me since we'd sent to him for help."

Astrid frowned. "The Mer King said something else strange when he came to rescue us. He asked if the princess was all right. Who was he talking about?"

I ground my teeth. Astrid was too smart. "He probably got his Fae nobility mixed up. He's a royal himself and probably mistakes Fae nobles as using the same titles."

She nodded and seemed to accept the answer. I was worried about what she'd say to her mother when we got back, though. I let it drop. There was no way of fixing what Patty might think.

Chip held up his phone and pointed at the approaching headlights across the marina parking lot. "That's our car. Come on. I'll feel a lot better when I'm home and in some clean and dry clothes."

We climbed in. I sat in the back between the girls while Chip rode up front with our driver. Chip made random conversation with the driver, like he always did with strangers we encountered. The girls looked out their respective windows and even dozed for the twenty-minute drive back to our place in Myrtle Beach.

When we pulled up out front of the duplex, Patty came running outside. She leaped from the top step of the front porch to the side-walk. Patty cupped her hands to her eyes and peered into the tinted windows, looking for her daughter.

Astrid popped open the door, and Patty pulled her into an embrace. "What were you thinking, running off like that? I was worried to death."

"Can we talk later? Miss Rose has already yelled at us. I don't need it from you, too." Astrid pushed her mother away and trudged up the steps to their side of the duplex.

Patty's eyes locked with mine. I nodded to confirm what her daughter had said. I was sure I'd get some sort of reprimand for talking to Astrid that way.

To my surprise, Patty said, "Rose should have yelled at you. And if you think you're just going to bed without giving me an explanation, you're sorely mistaken, young lady."

"Mom, I'm tired." Astrid's whiny voice chipped away at my composure.

I said, "Listen to your mother, Astrid. She's just worried about you."

Patty's tone shifted instantly. She turned on me. "I have this, Rose. Thank you."

I guess that was a step too far.

Patty marched up and gripped Astrid by the arm. She pushed her daughter into the open front door and turned back to Chip and me. "Can Clayton stay over with Addie the rest of the night? They're both asleep in his room."

Chip said, "Sure. You go deal with her. We'll send him over after breakfast in the morning."

Patty stalked inside and slammed the door shut behind her.

Sadie was almost inside the front door when I caught her slipping away. "Sadie, don't you dare think you're going up to your room before we talk more about this."

"Aunt Rose is right," Chip said. "We have a lot to talk about." He gestured for me to enter the house first, then he followed me inside, closing the front door.

Sadie flounced down on the couch with her arms crossed. "It was stupid. I already admitted we were wrong. Besides, it all worked out in the end."

I almost had to push my dropped jaw back up with my hand. It took me a second to come up with something that wasn't a string of curses. "It all worked out in the end only after your uncle and I raced out there to your rescue. There's someone out there hunting you right now, Sadie. Your little demonstration of power in that submarine only helped them home in on you. When our enemy gets here, I hope Conroy doesn't help them put two and two together."

Chip sat down on the other end of the couch. "We have to be careful, Sadie. The summer will be over in a few more weeks, and we'll have to go back to Maryland. There's a lot we have to do here before it's safe to go back home." He got up and walked over to the sink, where he poured himself some water from the filtered pitcher in the fridge. "We need some backup. Someone we can trust to come down here and help with watching Addy while your aunt and I help you get your power under control for good."

That caught me by surprise. "Who did you have in mind? Warren is in the middle of a project I gave him. He won't be able to drop things fast enough to get down here."

"I'll come up with someone." I opened my mouth to object. He added, "Someone you can trust. Don't worry, Rose, I understand what's at stake here." He had his phone out and tapped something into it before scrolling through the entries that popped up.

I couldn't see what he'd opened, and I didn't have much choice. I had to trust him. "If you say so, Chip. I hope tonight's events don't make Ben call off the debutante event next week. It's very important to Allura that our families formally connect before Sadie comes of age. We could use him in our corner over the next few years."

"We're still going?" Sadie asked. "I figured you'd tell me I was grounded and couldn't go."

I shook my head. "If it was just for you, I'd definitely ground you, but this is important to the whole family and your future coronation. You're going to attend and play the part asked of you. But that is it. We will be keeping you on a tight leash for the rest of this vacation, young lady."

"I'm not a dog. I have the right to do what I want."

"No," Chip said. "Actually, you don't. I remember when I was your age and thought I was grown-up enough to take care of myself. If anything, the events of earlier this evening proved you wrong. You'll follow instructions and do what is required at the party, then we're leaving. We're not going to this party for you to enjoy yourself. Consider it part of the work of becoming the Queen someday."

I appreciated Chip's show of support. I had been afraid he was going to cave and let Sadie's big sapphire eyes melt his heart.

"Go up to bed." I nodded at the stairs. "We're all tired. Chip and I will make the arrangements for what has to happen at the party, provided Ben hasn't changed his mind."

Sadie stood. The weariness was clear in her sagging shoulders and drooping head as she climbed the stairs. Once she was out of sight, I let out a long sigh. It was the first opportunity I'd had all night to let go of the tension in my body.

"I feel you," Chip said. "Tonight was the closest we've ever come to losing her. I hope the rest of her teen years won't be as bad. We might have to lock her up in her room for the foreseeable future."

That brought half a smile to my face as I remembered my own rebellious teen years. I had hoped Sadie would take after her mother and be the perfect daughter. I guess my help in raising the two kids had rubbed off some of my rougher side on her.

"It'll calm down some in a year or two. I seem to remember not fighting with Aunt Allura all the time at some point. I think it was around my fifteenth birthday."

"Two years?" Chip said. "I don't know if I can wait that long for this to go away."

"We'll just have to be our best suspicious selves until she settles down." I smiled. "Don't worry, Chip. I have your back. Let's get some sleep and tackle this fresh in the morning."

"Sounds like a great idea." He left his empty water glass in the sink and walked back toward his room. "Good night, Rose. You were great out there."

"So were you, Chip. Good night."

Chip

My alarm went off way too soon. Eminem's voice and a throbbing beat blared out from my phone beside the bed. I groaned and rolled over, pawing at the nightstand to shut it off. I finally found it lying on the wireless charger. Squinting at the screen through sleepy eyes, I tapped the stop icon to turn off the music.

I lay there and stared up at the ceiling, my mind recounting the events of the night before. One image kept returning to the top of my mind: Rose standing beside the submarine wearing next to nothing, a rusty pipe in her hand, ready to take on all comers to defend us. She had been spectacular during our rescue of the girls. She was always there for us—and me—when we needed her. I didn't let her know we appreciated her as much as I should. Maybe when we got back to Maryland, there'd be time to come up with a way to celebrate her contribution to our unusual family unit.

An aching pain stabbed my side as I sat up. I'd exercised muscles I rarely used in our underwater rescue last night, and the aftereffects had already started this morning. I didn't relish how sore I was going to be by the end of the day.

"Embrace the pain, Chip," Rose said from outside the doorway I'd left open in my sleepy stupor the night before. She held out a steaming mug of what I hoped was coffee. "I brewed a pot. We're going to need it this morning."

"I'm surprised to see you up so early," I said. Luckily, I'd fallen asleep in my shorts and t-shirt. I got up and took the offered coffee with a nod of thanks.

"The boys got up and started gaming again with the dawn. I can hear them cheering through the paper-thin walls. It's almost as if they're in my room with me."

I laughed. "You're a better aunt than I'd be. I'd have charged in there and told them to go back to sleep."

"Don't think I didn't consider it. Then I got up and started on breakfast."

That got my attention. "What are we having?"

"French toast, fried eggs, and country sausage," Rose replied. "I would've added some biscuits, too, but we don't have any baking ingredients."

"No worries, that all sounds delicious." I followed Rose out to the kitchen. The smell of the sausage filled the room. My mouth watered, and my stomach growled.

"Was that you?" Rose asked, staring at my stomach.

"What can I say? Underwater midnight rescues make me super hungry."

Rose picked up the tongs and worked on the sausage in the frying pan. "I'll finish up here. You can go tell the boys to stop the video games and come down. Roust out Sadie while you're at it. No reason she should get to sleep in this morning. I'm sure we can find some necessary chores to do around the house."

"Agreed. Heck, I'll make up some unnecessary ones if need be."

I sipped my coffee and went upstairs. The caffeine hadn't kicked in, and I winced when I opened the door to Addy's room and loud victory shouts washed over me. No wonder Rose had gotten up early.

"Hey, Uncle Chip," Addy said without taking his eyes off the flatscreen over the dresser. Both boys sat at the foot of the bed with their legs crossed, each holding a controller.

"Good morning. I'm glad you're having fun, but game time is over. Wrap up this battle round and come downstairs for breakfast."

"Aw, Uncle Chip, we're almost to the boss level."

"You heard me. The boss will still be there when you play the next time. When I come back down from waking Sadie, I expect the TV to be off." I waited for them each to nod before I left to go up to the third floor.

The doorknob to Sadie's room burned my palm. I hissed and yanked my hand away. My other hand rubbed at the blisters that had formed on my palm.

"What the…?" I didn't stop to answer my own question. Lowering my shoulder, I hit the door with everything I had. At the same time, I pressed out with my guardian barrier, expecting to find a roaring inferno, with flames all around me.

The door burst inward, and I stumbled inside Sadie's room. There were flames all right, but these flames were blue and green, and definitely magical in nature.

Sadie floated three feet above the mattress, her arms and legs out like a starfish.

"Rose, get up here!" I pressed against the wall of magic flames with my barrier. Despite the hot doorknob, the flames hit me like static electricity, not burning heat. My hair stood straight up from my scalp and all along my arms and exposed legs below my shorts.

My niece twisted, her head turning back and forth. I realized she was locked in a vivid nightmare.

"Sadie, honey, wake up," I called out. "You're dreaming." I shuffled forward, pressing against the magic trying to force me away.

"Whoa, that's awesome," Clayton said from the door.

Addy stood behind him, his jaw dropped open in awe.

I didn't have time to be nice. "Addy, get Clayton downstairs. Now!"

Rose appeared in the hall at the top of the stairs behind them. She grabbed the boys by their shoulders and hustled them to the steps. She told them something, but I couldn't hear what she said. The static in the air around me roared with energy.

With the boys sent away, Rose returned to the doorway. She moved her hands in an intricate pattern. Her emerald eyes flashed, and a pale green energy field formed in front of her. She pressed it forward and stepped toward me.

"Rose, she's having a nightmare. It's released her wild magic again."

She came up next to me and shouted over the roar of the energy storm around the bed. "That's not only her magic. Something else is at work here. We need to cut her off from the source."

I nodded. "If we work together, we might have a chance to isolate her. I'll slide around to the far side of the bed, then we'll press our magical fields forward like a clamshell around her."

"Go, I'll start here." Rose raised her arms, continuing the intricate dance with her hands.

I shuffled sideways, being careful to keep my guardian shield between me and Sadie. It seemed like an eternity, but within thirty seconds, I was in position.

Rose's glowing emerald eyes met mine, and we both nodded in unison.

I pressed forward, shaping the barrier into a shallow bowl shape, like a shell. I stretched the edges outward by spreading my arms wide to envelop Sadie's hovering body from my side.

Rose's green magic field elongated and formed a shape similar to mine. We both pressed forward, willing our edges to meet, starting with the side closest to Sadie's feet.

I let out a sigh as our fields met. A sensation of warmth and love filled me as our two magics connected. From the way Rose's eyes widened, she felt it, too.

There was no time to bask in the glow of our combined power. We had to keep up the pressure to cut off whatever power had reached out to Sadie. I let the sensation of comfort guide me as we sealed the edges of our barrier around the floating girl up past her waist, then her shoulders, finally completing the shell over her head.

The instant the field closed completely, Sadie's eyes opened, and she gasped. Then she dropped back onto the mattress.

The flames dissipated into a colorful mist. In less than a minute, they'd faded into nothingness.

"Aunt Rose, Uncle Chip. What happened?"

"You were dreaming," I said, "and some sort of magical energy wrapped around you."

Rose added, "What do you remember of the dream?"

"I was back in the submarine, but I was alone. Something waited for me there, and I tried to hide from it. The only way I knew to resist it was to release my wild magic and push it back."

Rose locked eyes with me. "He's found her."

"Are you sure?" I asked. I needed to believe Sadie was still safe. "She fought back with her magic and kept the one seeking her at bay in the dream. That means she succeeded, right?"

"That could explain why the flames were both blue and green." Rose reached out and brushed a stray stand of dark hair away from Sadie's face. "You're sure they didn't locate you in the dream? You remained hidden?"

"I'm sure. I'd remember if they'd found me. I could feel the hate and anger at wanting to get to where I was."

I shrugged. "They haven't come here. They're still searching at the submarine. That's a good sign."

"Believe me, Chip, we don't want anyone coming here. That would be a terrible sign."

Just then, Clayton called up from downstairs. "Mr. Chip, there's an exterminator here. They're snooping around on the front porch."

Rose's eyes went cold. My hand went to my waist until I realized my sword hilt was downstairs on my dresser with my wallet and keys.

"Stay here with Sadie, Rose. I'll go see who it is. It's probably a local homeless person or something."

"Dressed as an exterminator?" Rose asked.

I shrugged and started down the stairs. As I neared the first floor, Clayton and Addy were both clustered by the door, taking turns staring out of the peephole.

"Boys, get away from the door. It could be dangerous."

"The exterminator seems confused, Mr. Chip," Clayton said. "It's like he's not sure he's in the right place."

Something didn't make sense. I crossed the room to the front door. "How do you know it's an exterminator?"

Clayton smiled. "He's wearing a beekeeper's suit. I saw one once on a class field trip to a local farm."

"A beekeeper's suit?" That was strange.

I took a deep breath and decided to trust my instincts. Something told me there was no danger here. Maybe it was my Guardian senses, maybe it was my imagination. Either way, without peeking out first, I pulled open the door to confront the strange beekeeper.

The strange individual on the porch jumped up from their crouch and took a step backward. Their arms windmilled, and they almost fell off the top step.

I grabbed at the flailing hand closest to me to steady them.

They regained their balance, and a muffled voice said, "Chip, I wasn't sure this was the right place, and since it was early, I didn't want to wake anyone."

I knew that voice. "Cousin Gibbie? Is that you?"

"You said you needed help. Family is everything to me. I jumped in my van and came running."

"But why the outfit?" I gestured at the full beekeeper's regalia he wore.

He pointed to the sun rising low in the east and lighting the whole front porch. "It was the only way I could avoid that."

"Oh, right, the vampire thing. Come inside and take that off."

"Thank you. It's boiling inside here."

I moved aside and waved for Gibbie to tromp past me in his heavy canvas outfit, complete with booted overalls and a broad-brimmed hat with an opaque net hanging down around his head.

As soon as he got inside, my distant cousin pulled off the hat to reveal his sweaty, slightly balding head. "Whew, that's a relief. So, Chip, what do you need? Your message for help was vague, to say the least."

I opened my mouth to answer, but the words never came out. Rose's voice interrupted from the stairs.

"You called that one for help, Chip? Him? Really?"

The disapproval dripped from her tone, and it totally deflated Gibbie's proud stance.

"I can go if this isn't a good time." He fussed with the hat to pull it back into place before he ventured outside again.

"No, you stay. Rose, this is a family problem, and Gibbie is family. He's the right choice to be here. I'm the Guardian, and I know it."

I could tell from the look on Rose's face that she wasn't happy about me pulling rank on her.

"Fine, suit yourself. We've got hungry kids to feed and a malevolent evil somewhere nearby. I'm sure you've got everything under control."

The way she flipped her ponytail around like a whip told me she was finished talking. She strode into the kitchen to finish breakfast. All the closeness and warmth we'd felt upstairs washed away in an instant, replaced by the chill that usually existed between us.

Gibbie unzipped his heavy canvas overalls and tried to step out of them. He failed the dismount and fell to the floor, his arms and legs flailing. The two boys both laughed, and that set Gibbie giggling, too.

Before I knew it, I started laughing with them and Sadie joined in. Somehow, his arrival had changed the tone and reset the context of what we faced. It was hopeful now, and that was just what we needed.

25

Rose

Despite my initial reaction to Gibbie's arrival, I had to admit having Chip's vampire cousin around might be a good thing. Having another powerful Unusual on the team, even one as inept as Gibbie, gave me the freedom to focus on the preparations for the party with the Mer King.

Sadie didn't have any more episodes in her sleep over the next week. At least, there were none powerful enough to wake us up and require our help. Whatever Chip and I had done to seal off access to our niece had also had the added benefit of shielding our girl from whoever was searching for her. My mind drifted back to the warmth I'd experienced in that intimate magical moment of connection with Chip. Though I'd never tell him as much, it had stirred something inside I hadn't wanted to admit about my parenting counterpart.

I pushed away that thought as soon as it rose. There was no way I had any romantic interest in Chip Proctor. I had Fin for the time being to soothe my needs in that way. Even though we'd had a few bumpy moments, I felt a connection to the shark shifter I hadn't felt with another being in a very long time. I certainly wouldn't screw that up for another dalliance with Chip.

Of course, our summer at the beach was nearly over. We'd soon have to return to Westminster and the kids' normal lives. Sadie's wild magic still experienced small outbreaks, but Chip and I had worked with her on tamping down the emotional spikes. She was gaining control over her new and powerful connection.

As for Fin and me, once I left Myrtle Beach, we would be over. I held no illusions about him and his intentions, or my own. Neither of us were up for a long-distance relationship. For all I knew, I was simply Fin's summer tourist fling. It was better for me to focus on the events that were most important, and that included presenting Sadie to the Mer Court, albeit with her true identity disguised. The Mer King would know and, when the time was right after her coronation in a few years, he would reveal to his folk that he'd known who she was all along.

Sadie's big night approached quickly. The summer dresses were bought, and Gibbie settled into a regular routine, watching Addy and Clayton in the afternoons and evenings while all three played video games together. Chip's cousin would watch over the house and the boys while Chip and I accompanied Sadie to the party down on Myrtle's Grand Strand. Strangely, Patty didn't have hangups about letting a vampire watch Clayton. Apparently, Chip's vouching for the babysitter was all she needed.

On the big night, Patty waited out front with Astrid, who looked lovely in her pale green sundress with a delicate wreath of summer flowers in her hair. The arrangement almost gave the impression of a tiara, and I couldn't help but wonder if that was what Patty was going for. The insufferable woman had acted strangely ever since the trip to rescue the girls from the submarine.

I walked down from the porch to where they waited by Chip's SUV. "You both look lovely. I like the flowery tiara, Astrid."

"Doesn't it look positively regal, Rose?" Patty said. "You know, our family has ancestors from the old Fae royal line."

I shrugged. "Most Fae nobles do." How I looked forward to rubbing her nose in this when Sadie took the throne.

"It's a shame Sadie can never claim that connection, not truly."

I glared at Patty. "What's that supposed to mean?"

"I not trying to be offensive, Rose, but surely her half-human side dilutes her connection to any sort of claim like Astrid has."

Astrid said, "Mother, you're being rude."

Patty smirked. "I'm only speaking the truth. It's actually quite the concession that the Mer King included her in tonight's presentation ceremony at all."

My fists bunched up at my sides. What was it about this woman that got under my skin so easily? Picturing a grown Sadie with all the royal regalia around her, I blew out a long breath and released the tension.

The door behind us opened, and Sadie came out in her knee-length blue dress. Chip beamed with pride behind her. I couldn't blame him. She looked lovely. Our little girl was definitely growing up.

"Ready, ladies?" Chip asked. He waggled his keys. "Time to get on the road. I still don't know why we don't just walk. It's only a few blocks down the Strand."

"Not in these shoes, Chip," I said. My heels already had my feet aching. I wore my own summer dress in pale lavender. I lamented not having a way to wear my blade, but I'd stashed it in the SUV in case I needed it.

Patty smiled. "Good thing we women run things in this family, right, Rose?"

Whose family was she talking about? Rather than fight with her, I nodded and gestured to the vehicle. "Shall we load up?"

Chip opened the front passenger door, and I slipped past Patty and sat up front before she could come over and climb in. "Thank you, Chip." Yes, it was petty, but you had to take the minor victories in things like this.

Patty humphed and climbed in the back with the two girls. Astrid sat in the middle, while Sadie sat behind the driver's seat. I realized my mistake as an itch settled in between my shoulder blades. Patty sat directly behind me. Not that she'd do anything to me worse than glare at the back of my head, but I never liked putting my back at any enemy, no matter how innocuous.

"Ready?" Chip asked as he pulled away from the curb. "Time for the big party."

"You should be in for a treat, Chip," Patty said. "Humans rarely get invited to events like this."

"It's a summer party to get with the local bigwigs," Chip said. "I'm sure that will include some of the local human leaders who know about the existence of Unusuals."

"Perhaps," Patty said. "Still, you should understand how big a night this is for some of us."

Chip glanced in the rearview mirror at Patty. "What do you mean?"

"After what happened in the girls' underwater excursion, I reached out to a local oracle, Adella's grandmother. I wanted to confirm something Astrid mentioned that the shark boy had said down there."

Astrid glared at her mom. "Mother, we don't need to make a big deal out of this."

"But it is a big deal, my dear," Patty said. "The oracle foretold the presentation of a visitor who would be the next Fae queen. She claimed it would occur before this summer's end."

Chip's eyes met mine before he returned his attention to the road. This wasn't good. I said, "Why would you go to an oracle about something like that? There hasn't been a Fae queen for five hundred years. Certainly, the old royal line is now defunct, no matter what the old legends say."

"I certainly thought so, too, until this summer. I'm bursting to tell someone what I learned."

I tensed in the front seat. "What was that?" Had the oracle revealed Sadie's true identity?

"My Astrid is destined to be the next queen of the Fae."

Chip let out a stifled snort.

My jaw dropped. "I'm sorry. What?"

"It's the only thing that makes sense. The shark boy said something to Astrid about a powerful Fae down there. The old Mer King even asked after a princess' safety. It all makes sense. Astrid is evidencing the powers of royalty. At first I thought the flares I felt had come from Sadie, but that's ridiculous, given her heritage. She could never manifest anything that powerful. All the signs point to Astrid, of course."

Rage welled up within me for a second. I quickly tamped it down.

Turning around and belting her wouldn't solve anything. As if Patty Peyton couldn't be more insufferable.

"That's wonderful news," Chip said.

I twisted in my seat to glare at Chip.

He gave me one of his beaming grins. "I'm serious, Rose. I don't know much about such things, but if Astrid's some sort of royalty, I'm happy for them both."

"Thank you, Chip," Patty said. "It really is such a big deal. I haven't had enough time to fully process it myself."

I glanced over my shoulder at Sadie. She sat behind Chip. Her face blazed as red as mine probably was. This got under her skin, too, and that might not be a good thing. If this brought out one of Sadie's outbursts, we'd have to explain it to Patty.

"You know what, Sadie?" I said. "This is great news. All eyes will be on Astrid at the event tonight. You never like getting any attention, right?" Word of what the oracle had said would slip out somehow to the assembled nobles. Since Sadie had never met the oracle, she didn't have a specific vision. It also meant that Adella hadn't revealed to her grandmother whatever she saw in my aura that first day we met at the beach.

In response to my announcement, Sadie gave a jerky nod. "Of course, Aunt Rose. Astrid, that's great news. I'm happy for you." She forced a smile that seemed to fool Patty and Astrid, but not me. This hurt her inside.

Chip said, "We're almost there. Should I pull up in front of the pavilion and let the four of you out, or do you want to walk over from the parking lot with me?"

"Out front," Patty said.

"We'll walk," I chimed in simultaneously.

"Okay, then." Chip rolled his eyes and turned left. He pulled in next to a large, enclosed pavilion. The sign out front said, *Closed for Private Party*. "I'll drop anyone who wants out first."

Patty popped open her door and stepped down to the sidewalk. Astrid slid over behind her. To my surprise, Sadie followed her. I guess that meant I was getting out here, too.

"Wait for me." I hopped down to stand beside Sadie. "Shall we?" I placed my hand at the small of Sadie's back to guide her forward.

She shrugged her shoulders and stepped away, closer to Astrid. "I can walk myself in."

I caught the quick correction in her tone. This wasn't the place to take offense. Besides, it had to sting hearing Patty's announcement about Astrid. Better to let her be alone with her thoughts for the time being. She was no longer red-faced with anger. That meant there was less risk of a wild magic outbreak.

Chip pulled away with the SUV. Patty walked up the two steps to the concrete floor of the street pavilion. A pop cover band jammed on the stage across the space. There were already dozens of people there. I didn't see Ben, the Mer King. He'd probably make his own special entrance once the later arrivals had shown up.

Mills bounced over, followed by the bashful Adella. Both wore pretty dresses of their own. Words spilled from the young werewolf girl in a rush. "Hey, you both look great! Astrid, I saw your text about the news. That's amazing! Congratulations! Should I curtsy or something?"

Astrid laughed, and flipped her hair back when several other young girls her age came over. "No, it's not like I'm the queen yet. I have to turn eighteen first. You can call me Princess if you want."

"Princess it is," Mills said. "I can't believe I'll be able to say I know you. What's it like?"

Adella stood behind Mills and frowned but didn't say anything to let out the secret she knew.

Astrid laughed. "I'm still just me. I've always thought I was special and meant for something great."

Behind Astrid, the flush started creeping up toward Sadie's face from her bare shoulders. I slid over, letting Patty and Astrid handle the gaggle of girls who'd come to bask in the presence of supposed greatness.

"Come on." I tugged at Sadie with a gentle nudge. "Let's go get some punch and see who else is here."

She took the hint and walked beside me to the refreshment table.

"Aunt Rose, I don't think I want to be here anymore. Can we go home?"

"No, kiddo. This is one of those things we have to do. You have to be formally presented to the Mer King. He's big on propriety, and we owe him that much after he came to your rescue down in the submarine. Besides, don't you look forward to the day when Astrid finds out the truth? That will be epic revenge."

I used a ladle to dip some red punch into a plastic up. I sipped it. It didn't seem to be spiked with any alcohol, so I dipped some for Sadie and handed her the cup.

"Here, drink this and remember to smile. No matter how you feel inside, we need to keep up appearances."

Sadie took a drink and nodded toward Astrid and all those gathered around. "Sometimes I don't know why I like her so much. There are so many things she does that infuriate me."

Across the pavilion, Chip entered and looked around until he spotted Sadie and me.

"Believe me, Sadie. I know exactly what you mean. I think you'll work it out, though. It's not like Astrid can announce this at school in a few weeks. No one who knows anything about this event is there. You're just normal human girls to your other friends."

"Yeah, but Astrid always seems to come out on top, even there." Sadie frowned. "It's not fair."

"Come on, let's go listen to the band. They're pretty good and maybe they take requests. I'll bet if we find the right song, we'll get your uncle to dance."

Sadie giggled. "That would be funny."

With her mood changed for the time being, the two of us moved over to the side of the stage and listened while the band played. Chip joined us, his head bobbing to the steady beat. I caught Sadie's eye and winked. We might just get our wish after all.

26

Chip

The first thing I noticed as I entered the enclosed pavilion was the band. For a cover band, they were better than just good. The lead singer, a woman with pale green streaks in her long blonde hair, entranced me with her clear, melodic voice. I detoured from joining Rose and Sadie by the refreshment table to get a closer look, her crooning drawing me closer.

I stood there for a while, nodding along with the beat, unable to pull my eyes away from the woman behind the microphone. She seemed to sing only for me, meeting my gaze with her piercing blue eyes.

A sharp tug on my elbow, followed by a slap to the back of my head, jerked me away from the bandstand.

"What the hell, Rose?" I wrenched my attention from the mesmerizing voice to direct my anger at my sister-in-law. "I was listening to that song."

She rolled her eyes and pointed at my collarbone. "Reach up and touch that precious shark's tooth around your neck. You're being entranced by magic."

"There's no way that I'm…" My words trailed off as my fingers pressed the gold shark's tooth where it lay between my t-shirt and button-down shirt. It usually lay against my bare skin, but it had settled outside the undershirt this time.

Biting cold nipped my fingers through the outer shirt. There was definitely magic at play here, and the charm should have protected me from it, except it wasn't in direct contact with me. I unbuttoned the next button so I could reach it and slip the magical Guardian charm back inside my t-shirt.

My mind cleared the instant the cold metal settled against my chest. I twisted to stare at the singer. She was pretty good, but nowhere near as good as I'd thought only moments before. How had she done that?

"She's a siren, Chip. They used to lure lonely sailors to them along rocky shores all over the world. Their voices are powerful and enticing when they want to be. She should know better than to try something like that here, but maybe she was just having some fun." Rose looked me in the eye. "You better now?"

"Yeah, I'm good. Thanks for the heads up. There's still a lot I need to learn about you Unusuals, I guess."

Rose gave me a playful nudge with her elbow. "That's the first time you've admitted to needing my help in a while, Chip. Thank you."

"We're a team. I couldn't do any of the things I do raising the kids and navigating this Unusual world without your help."

"Good," she said and nodded. "Don't you forget it. Now we need to monitor Sadie and distract her from Patty and Astrid. They're holding court over there, acting as if they're the real royal family."

"To be fair to Patty," I said, "she really believes it." I don't know why I felt the need to defend Patty in that moment, but it was a mistake.

Rose rounded on me. "Don't lose sight of the true mission here, Chip. We can't have the Mer King think there's any doubt about the succession."

"How do we do that when we can't publicly declare Sadie for who she is?"

Rose tugged me to follow her to where Sadie stood chatting with Adella and Mills. She leaned in to whisper to me before we got there. "I don't know. I'll think of something. In the meantime, keep Sadie distracted from Astrid and her mom. This is not the place for her wild magic to escape."

I followed Rose over to join the three girls.

Adella said, "It was a shock when my grandma had that vision. She hasn't been herself since it happened, though."

"I hope she's okay," Sadie said. Genuine concern filled her voice.

"A foretelling of great portent like this takes a lot of power from the seer involved. She just needs some rest. She's not coming tonight because of it. I'll have to fill her in on all the drama with Astrid when I get home."

Mills added, "It's pretty cool that we've been hanging out with Fae royalty all summer and didn't even know it."

Sadie shrugged. "Royals are people just like us. It's no big deal, really."

"It's a huge deal," Mills replied. "She'll have great power someday. At least, that's what I've heard. There's so much we don't know about your people. It's been a long time since you had a queen."

"I'm just saying, Astrid's the same girl she was earlier this summer. Besides, it could all be a mistake."

Adella shook her head. "All my grandmother said was the future Fae queen is here in Myrtle Beach and will be presented to the Mer King tonight."

Mills sneered. "I mean, it's not like it's you, Sadie. No offense. Astrid explained to me about your dad being human and all."

Sadie's face and shoulders flushed red. She opened her mouth to say something.

Rose jumped in before she could speak. "I think that's enough speculation about people's past and heritage. That's not something any of us should talk about, right?"

"You're right, Miss Rose." Mills reached out and took Sadie's hand in hers. "I'm sorry, Sadie. I was out of line. Forgive me?"

It took Sadie a second to answer. She'd let her attention shift to watching Astrid and her mother across the room with a collection of local Unusual leaders clustered around them.

"Uh, yeah, there's nothing to forgive. After all, my father was human. You weren't lying."

The band shifted to a driving dance beat, and Mills hopped in place and reached out for Sadie and Mills. "Come on. I love this song. Let's dance. This is a party, and we should have fun."

The tall blonde werewolf teen bounded to the center of the dance floor in front of the stage. Sadie and Adella laughed and followed her. Soon, all three lost themselves in the gyrations of their own personal dance moves.

"Crisis averted," I said to Rose. She watched the girls with a cautious glare.

"It's a long night. Stay on your toes. I have a feeling something is going to happen."

"Do you sense a threat?" I asked. I glanced around while I rested my hand on the collapsed tube of the sword hilt clipped to my belt.

"No, it's more of an itch between my shoulders I can't scratch. Something is looming. I just don't know what."

The band finished the song, and the keyboard player blasted out a fanfare of trumpets.

The lead singer leaned into her mic and said, "Ladies and Gentlemen of the Unusual community, please direct your attention to the entrance for our host this evening, his Majesty Benedict Karmilo, master of the rolling deep, and overlord of the Atlantic Mer Folk."

Rose and I moved over to stand with Sadie and the other two girls. The double doors opened, and in walked the one we knew as Ben, though he didn't resemble the simple arcade owner we'd first met. He wore a suit that sparkled with iridescent blues and greens. The colors shifted as he walked, and the lights made the fabric sparkle with the different shades of his outfit.

Beside him walked Benni. Her simple white sundress was trimmed with the same blue and green shimmering effect of her grandfather's suit. She smiled and nodded at the people she passed as they approached the stage. Her grandfather helped her up the steps to the bandstand before following her.

Ben stepped up to the mic. "Welcome, welcome, one and all. It is my great pleasure to present my granddaughter and heir, Benedicta. In her honor, I will receive all the fair young ladies of a similar age. Each will pass and receive our goodwill and blessing."

The line formed by the left-hand steps as if by magic. Astrid stood in the middle of the line while Patty fussed over her. I could tell by Patty's face that she thought Astrid should go first. The girls in the front part of the line weren't giving up their spots, though.

I followed Sadie over as she took a spot near the end of the line. Adella stood behind her and Mills in front. Rose and I hovered nearby. There were a few parents standing beside their children in the line. Most, however, stood in a group facing the stage, their phones ready to capture the moment when their youngling passed by the Mer King in his official position over the local Unusual community.

The young ladies approached Ben and Benni, one at a time. A commotion back by the entrance drew my attention away from the stage. I twisted around to see what was up.

Fin had staggered in. He was a bloody mess, his blue jeans and t-shirt soaked in blood from gashes on his arms and chest.

Rose gasped and ran to him, helping him stand when his knees buckled from his injuries.

"Fin, what happened to you?" Rose asked. "Is all this blood yours?"

"Not all of it, but enough." His ragged voice was interspersed with rattling coughs.

I could tell he was bleeding internally from the foamy blood in his mouth. I lifted my phone. "I should call an ambulance. You need a hospital. Why did you come here?"

"No time. You have to get everyone away from here. They're right behind me."

I looked around.

Rose beat me to the question. "Who is right behind you?"

"A new power is trying a takeover of some sort. They supported my opponents for control of the Shark community. I couldn't stop them, and they've somehow influenced the entire school to come to their side. Get away. They mentioned your niece by name, along with the other visiting Fae girl."

Rose straightened. "Chip, get Sadie out of the line and go to the SUV. Don't stop for anything. I'll do what I can for Fin here and try to slow them down."

"What about Patty and Astrid?" I asked. "They're coming for her, too."

Rose shook her head. "I'll warn her. You get Sadie to safety. She's your responsibility."

She was right. I ran over to the back of the line. Only a few of the people had even noticed Fin's entrance. All other eyes were on the front of the pavilion. The line had moved up onto the stage, each girl talking with the king for a moment before continuing off to the other side.

"Sadie, come with me." I reached out to grab her hand.

She pulled it back out of reach. "Why? We've done so much to prepare for today. I want my turn, too."

"You'll get your turn. Just not now." I reached for her again, and she stepped back.

Sadie focused over my shoulder, and her blood drained away, leaving her pale as a ghost.

I looked back. A shadowed figure had entered the pavilion. A group of thirty bulky and muscular shark shifters spread out around the ominous central shadow-person. I tried to pierce the veil of darkness that hid the face in the shadows of a black cloak.

"Stop!" The shadow man bellowed the order. His voice filled the entire room. "Turn over the two Fae girls to me. They will not receive the king's blessing. They are mine."

Ben stood and shouted into the microphone. "You dare to come here and interrupt this special event? Who do you think you are?" He held out his hand, and the silver and gold trident he had wielded in his arcade appeared in his right hand.

The shadow parted, and a long, pale finger pointed at the stage. "You are not the only one here who commands the ancient powers, old one. I am your better and will end you if you interfere. I have no quarrel with you. Take your kin and leave."

Ben leaped off the stage. He held his trident leveled at his side, the three barbed tines facing the shadow man. "This is my place, interloper. Feel my wrath."

White and pale-blue bands of energy shot out from the end of the trident.

The shadows absorbed the released energy. Instead of the light driving the shadows away, the shadows spread outward, as if fueled by the wild magic energy released by the Mer King.

The pale hand pointed back at Ben, and a jet of pure black smoke fired from his extended finger. Dark energy struck the Mer King in the chest before he could bring his trident up to block it. The blow knocked him backward. He slid across the floor until the edge of the stage stopped him. Black energy enveloped his crumpled form.

That broke the hold that had kept the crowd frozen in place.

Someone screamed. People bolted for the nearest exits, all trying to escape the fight. It appeared their king was losing, and no one wanted to remain here to be next.

Benni yelled and ran over to her grandfather to help him rise.

Adella and Mills ran for the side exit beside the stage with the others from the line. It was time for us to do the same.

Patty stood with Astrid behind her. She backed away from four approaching shark men. Their gaping human mouths were open and filled with rows of shark teeth. There was nothing I could do to help her. I had other priorities.

"Sadie, come on." I pulled her arm and bumped into the teen shark, Conroy.

Before I could react, he punched me in the chest. The pure force behind the blow caught me by surprise. I flew backward and crashed into the wall. My left arm bent beneath me, and a crack reverberated up through my shoulder. I was pretty sure it was broken.

I pushed up to my feet and unclipped the tubular hilt from my belt. I extended the blade until my sword was ready to defend Sadie.

"You leave her be." I ran at the shark boy. I didn't want to kill him, but that was up to him.

Conroy had grabbed Sadie by her shoulders and was pulling her back toward the shadow man. He laughed at me.

"Stay back, old man. The master only wants to talk with her and the other one."

A slender form streaked in from the side to tackle Conroy to the floor.

"Run, Sadie," Rose called out while wrestling with the young shark shifter.

I did the only thing I could think of doing. Sadie needed a distraction to make her escape. I charged the shadow man, my sword held high.

The pale arm that had been pointing at the crumpled form of the incapacitated Mer King swung around to point in my direction. A dark power blast came at me.

Everything stopped. I toppled, muscles frozen, to the floor.

27

Rose

Conroy's shifter strength proved almost more than I could handle. We rolled on the floor, each of us trying to gain the advantage. I didn't just have to avoid getting pinned down by the shark man. I also had to keep the snapping teeth away.

After a few seconds, Conroy shouted in triumph as he rolled me over onto my back and straddled my waist. He pinned me with his hands pressing down on my upper arms.

"You'll regret challenging the master. He has power you can never match."

I had limited options in my position. "Right now, the only power I have to match is yours."

"Struggle all you wa—" The last word ended in a strangled scream as I brought my knee up hard into his crotch, driving his family jewels up into his gut with the force of my blow.

Conroy let go of my arms. His hands clutched at his groin.

I bucked once with my hips and pitched him to the side. My legs came up, and I rolled backward on my shoulders and kicked my legs to flip up to my feet.

A few feet away, Chip stood frozen in place, his entire form enveloped in a crackling, black magical field. No color escaped the shadow magic. Chip's pale face and clothing were all covered in shades of gray.

The sword had dropped from his grasp. I jumped forward and scooped it up. It was heavier than I was used to, but it would have to do since my blade was in Chip's SUV.

Sadie stood five feet away in front of the dark stranger, staring up into the darkness that shrouded his face. Two shark shifters brought a struggling Astrid over to stand beside her.

"Sadie, step back and come here." I reached out with my free hand. "Come on. Bring Astrid with you and get behind me."

"Quiet, Elf girl," the shadow figure said. "I should have dealt with you in Scotland. I won't make the same mistake again."

I barked a laugh. "You'll try. I'm ready for you this time."

"That sword won't stop me. I can sense the power in it, and it is not tuned to you. It belongs to a Guardian as of old, and yet somehow it was in the possession of that weak human."

"Let him go and see how weak he is." I needed to keep him talking. If he focused on me, he wasn't paying attention to Sadie. I hoped she'd take the chance to make a break for one of the exits. The shark shifters had moved to stand beside and behind the shadow man.

"I might, but only after I deal with these two Fae girls. One of them is the being I seek. The other means nothing to me. I have waited too long to let this moment pass because of further distractions."

I took a single step forward, and the crackling dark magic sprung up around me. It froze me in place like Chip, and I couldn't move, even to speak. The taste of the magic had a hint of wild magic amidst the darkness. It also felt the way Aunt Allura had described the old magic, that mythical power the Fae had possessed in the great forests before the humans harvested them all for lumber.

The dark figure stepped forward to loom over Sadie and Astrid. The shadow hood turned to face each, starting with Astrid. He stopped when he considered Sadie.

"Curious. This one has the odor of human blood. I wouldn't have thought it possible for one such as you to contain the power I have felt coming from this place." He leaned forward and sniffed the air a few inches over Sadie's head before straightening.

He sniffed the air again, and the pale hand came up and pointed at Astrid. "This one is pure blood. It must be her."

Patty lay against the wall to one side. Her leg bent underneath her at an impossible angle. There was no way for her to stand. She reached out with a pleading hand. "No, she's just a girl."

"I mean her no harm. It is the energy inside her I want. She will become queen and wield great power. Once I have taken her royal mana for myself, I will give her shell back to you."

Patty pulled at the floor, inching her shattered body closer to her daughter. "You can't take her inner power without killing her. Please, take it from me. I'm her mother. Surely, some of her power must reside in me as well."

The pointed finger stretched to Patty, and the dark energy crackled around her as well, stopping her forward motion.

"Your mother pleads your case well, girl. What do you have to say? Should I drain your mother's power first?"

Astrid shrieked and shook her head. "No, don't hurt her."

"Then it must be you, girl. Don't worry. You'll only feel the pain in the beginning."

The hand extended to hover over Astrid's head. Her face tilted upward, and her mouth opened in a silent wail. Pale wisps of blue energy escaped from her open eyes and mouth. The shadowy hand absorbed the released power.

"You will not hurt her!" Sadie's scream of rage caught me by surprise.

"Silence, half-blood." More of the crackling black energy enveloped Sadie. The shadow man turned his attention back to Astrid, assuming Sadie had frozen like the others.

Unnoticed by him, her left hand twitched and then reached out, ever so slowly, until it grasped Astrid's rigid hand beside her.

Bright blue light lit up Sadie's eyes. Seconds later, a similar blue nimbus spread from their clasped hands to surround Astrid. Sadie said, "Use your magic, Astrid. Defend us."

The pale blue energy floating in wisps from Astrid stopped. The bright sapphire-blue power now coursing around her cut off the shadow man's attack.

"What is this?" The shadow man's confusion betrayed a hint of fear. "How is this possible?"

The sapphire-blue energy changed to the blue-white of lightning. Astrid raised her hand, looking at her palm with a quizzical expression. A savage smile crossed her face. She stretched her hand toward the shadow man. A blast of the blue lightning power struck the shadow man in his chest, flinging him back ten feet to land on his ass on the floor. The shark men scattered away from him as he struggled to rise.

The fall broke his concentration, and the crackling energy drained away from others he'd affected. Chip and I dropped forward to the floor, gasping while we recovered our stolen strength. The same happened by the stage where the power had trapped the Mer King and Benni.

Ben regained his strength more quickly. "Enough! You dare to come here and harm my invited guests? Then feel the rage of the rolling deep."

The Mer King beckoned. His trident slid across the floor and popped up to land in his outstretched hand. Power jolted from the three tines. Instead of the white and blue bands of power Ben had wielded before, a deep, midnight-blue ray the color of the deepest ocean waters lanced out at the shadow man's chest.

This time, he couldn't counter the incoming force, and the blow sent him rolling across the floor, taking down several of the shark shifters milling around behind him.

Sadie and Astrid strode forward, still holding hands. They walked in tandem, almost as if of one mind. Astrid held out her free hand and said, "In the name of the once and future queen, I banish you back to whence you came."

I didn't know where Sadie or Astrid had learned the ancient curse. Another lance of the sapphire-blue power blasted from Astrid's hand and struck the crouching figure on the floor.

This time, it didn't fling the man away. Instead, it closed around him like a lead blanket, crushing him into a smaller and smaller version of himself. The dark figure folded in on himself, ever shrinking. Eventually, the last hint of shadow at the core of the blazing blue power winked out. The assembled shark shifters shared a few quick glances. After a few hurried nods between them, they ran from the pavilion.

Astrid lowered her arm. "Where did he go?"

I got to my feet and walked over to the girls. "He was a projection of power. He wasn't really here in person." I shook my head, realizing that was how he evaded my magic when I encountered him in Scotland.

Astrid looked down at her palm, flexing her fingers. "How did I do that? Did all that power come from me?"

Sadie leaped to answer before anyone else. "I think it must have been inside you all along."

"But I've never felt anything like it before. It was… exhilarating."

"You are the future queen! I knew it," Astrid's mother exclaimed. Joy brought tears to her eyes.

Astrid ran to Patty. She sat on the floor, nursing her broken leg. "You think so, mother? The seer wasn't completely sure."

"This proves it. You're really her." Patty pulled Astrid into her arms.

Behind her, Ben met my eyes.

I shrugged and nodded my consent to continue with the charade. This was better than exposing Sadie.

Ben moved to stand beside Astrid. "I am proud to be the first to have met and fought side by side with the next Fae queen. Long let the alliance between the Fae and Mer royal houses prevail."

A smattering of applause coursed around the room from the few who hadn't fled during the initial attack. People moved in to join Ben, Astrid, Patty, and Benni near the stage.

I put my arm around Sadie and whispered, "You were very brave. Ben knows what you did, and he won't forget."

"I know, Aunt Rose, but this doesn't feel right. I don't think Astrid and Miss Patty are going to let this pass quietly."

I let out a wry chuckle. "No, I don't think it's in Patty's nature to do that."

"Aunt Rose is right." Chip had come up on Sadie's opposite side. He cradled his broken arm in his other hand. "Now you can focus on growing up and being a normal teenager. Isn't that what you wanted anyway?"

"I thought so, but now that I see what that power brings, I want it, too."

"That's normal," I said. "Don't worry, your time will come soon enough. I can't wait to see the look on Patty's face when that revelation happens." Inside, I packed away that thought to cushion the next few years. Patty would be insufferable, lording Astrid's ascension to royalty over the rest of us.

Fin limped over to join us. "You all look like you weathered that well enough." He pointed at Chip's arm. "We should get you to the hospital, though."

Chip smiled. "Once again, I find myself wishing I had the regenerative powers of you shifters."

I retrieved Chip's sword from the floor and handed it to him. "I'll take the keys. You can't drive with that arm. We'll have you patched up in no time."

The four of us left the pavilion, and with it, the small celebratory crowd clustered around the one they thought was the next Fae queen. It was a bittersweet moment, but necessary to ensure Sadie lived to see the throne for real in five short years. I could wait. There was a lot that could happen between now and then. Chip and I would be ready for it, though. That much was certain. After all, he was the Guardian, and I'd be there to make sure he did his job right.

28

Chip

"Come on, kids, time to load up." I picked up the final suitcase with my one good arm and slid it into the rear of my SUV.

Sadie and Addison ran out of the duplex and down the steps. "Shotgun!" they yelled in unison. They both reached for the front passenger door at the same time.

"Sorry, kids. That seat is taken," I said.

Rose stood up from where she leaned on the hood. "Yep, I'm driving. Your Uncle Chip is riding shotgun."

"What about your Firebird, Aunt Rose?" Sadie asked. She looked up and down the street. "Where is it?"

"Fin parked it at his house. He'll keep an eye on it for me for a while. I'll fly down from Maryland in a week or so to pick it up."

I frowned. "I don't know why you insisted on driving us back. I still have one good arm."

"Traffic will be heavy. Besides, my car will be fine down here for a bit until I can come and fetch it. You can navigate if you insist on being helpful."

I didn't want to argue with her. This plan had the added benefit of giving her an excuse to come back down and see Fin without having the kids nearby as a distraction. She deserved that.

Gibbie waddled out through the front door in his bulky beekeeper's outfit. He hit the top porch step sooner than expected, and his arms windmilled to keep his balance. Somehow, he only stumbled down the three steps to the sidewalk and did not fall on his face.

He struck a pose in a half-crouch. "Wow, that was a close one. Look at me with the cat-like reflexes."

I laughed along with the kids at their vampire cousin's antics. "Thanks for coming down here on short notice. We appreciate it."

"Family first, Chip. Besides, I need to get away from Elk City more. You all give me a reason to travel from time to time." He hitched at the awkward canvas coveralls protecting him from the blaring noon sunlight overhead. "I need to get into my van and crank up the air conditioning. This outfit is too hot."

I extended a hand. "See you, Gibbie. Be careful driving home."

Gibbie took my hand and shook it with a firm grip. "It won't be so bad. I can strip out of this once I'm safely behind the window tinting. Plus, it'll be dark by the time I get back home."

He waved and got in his beat-up white van. A minute later, the engine started, sputtered a couple times, and belched black exhaust from the tailpipe. The van lurched into motion and pulled away from the curb.

I walked up and locked the duplex's front door. "Load up, folks," I said, returning to the SUV. "We're burning daylight."

Rose got in the front behind the wheel and started the engine.

I buckled in and twisted around to ensure the kids were buckled up, too. With a wave of my hand, I said, "Home, Rosie."

"Don't call me Rosie." She stepped on the gas and pulled away from our summer vacation home. It had served us well.

Sadie said, "I wish I could have said goodbye to Astrid. She's hardly been home in the two days since the party. I wanted to spend one more day on the beach with her."

"She's busy now," Rose said. "Everyone with any kind of connection to the local Fae nobility is fawning over both her and Miss Patty right now. That's good for us. It will distract attention from you for a little while longer."

Addison crossed his arms. "It's not fair, Aunt Rose. Sadie is the real queen. She should not be getting to have all that fun."

"Her turn will come, Addy," I said. "Your aunt is right. We don't need that kind of focus on you two. Enjoy the time to grow up a little more before the entire world wants all your attention."

I caught the hint of a nod from Rose. She approved. Maybe that made up for the "Rosie" comment. Or maybe not. It was hard to say with her.

I leaned back and watched the road ahead. We were eight hours from home and only a week away from school starting again. One more year of middle school, and then all we had to do was get our girl through high school in one piece. It couldn't be that hard, right?

Be ready for more coming in July 2025 with *Sophomore Fae, Book 5 in Uncle Chip Saves the Fae.*

Also by Jamie Davis

**Get a free book and updates for new books.
visit JamieDavisBooks.com/send-free-book/**

Extreme Medical Services Series

(A 9-book Urban Fantasy series starting with)

Book 1 - Extreme Medical Services

—

Eldara Sister Series

The Nightingale's Angel

Blue and Gray Angel

—

Lone Wolf Squadron Series

(a 9-book Space Western series starting with)

Marshal the Stars

—

The Huntress Clan Saga

(A 6-book Urban Fantasy series starting with)

Huntress Initiate

—

The Broken Throne Series

(A 5-Book Dystopian Urban Fantasy

starting with)

The Charm Runner

—

The Accidental Traveler LitRPG Series

(with C.J. Davis)

(A 6-book Epic Fantasy Series starting with)

The Accidental Thief

—

Follow on Facebook for updates, news, and upcoming book excerpts

Jamie's Fun Fantasy Readers Facebook Group

Help the Author

I Need Your Help ...

Without reviews indie books like this one are almost impossible to market.

Leaving a review will only take a minute — it doesn't have to be long or involved, just a sentence or two that tells people what you liked about the book, to help other readers know why they might like it, too. It also helps me write more of what you love.

The truth is, VERY few readers leave reviews. Please help me out by being the exception.

Thank you in advance!

Jamie Davis

About the Author

Jamie Davis writes stories where magic meets heart and family saves the day.

A nurse, retired paramedic, and lifelong gamer, Jamie brings a deep love of sci-fi, fantasy, and found family to every tale he tells—whether it's an enchanted road trip, a demon-possessed soccer ball, or a suburban uncle navigating fae politics with a toddler in tow. His books mix real-world emotion with wild, magical twists, and always leave room for a laugh (or a heartfelt tear).

When he's not writing or rolling dice, Jamie lives in the woods of Maryland with his wife, their three kids, and a dog who thinks she's the real hero of the story. He's the creator of Fun Fantasy Reads, a growing collection of novels across urban fantasy, LitRPG, sci-fi, and contemporary paranormal genres.

Jamie loves connecting with fans at cons and online—so don't be shy. Visit JamieDavisBooks.com for new releases, free stories, and more chances to escape into adventure.

Follow Jamie Online

facebook.com/jamiedavisbooks

instagram.com/podmedic